Smidge of Love

The Sunshine Breakfast Club
(Book 5)

KARICE BOLTON

This is a work of fiction. Names, places, incidents, and events either are the author's imagination or are used fictitiously. Any resemblance to actual persons, living or dead, events, or locales is entirely coincidental.

ISBN: 979-8-9872814-8-2

Cover Design by Didi Wahyudi

Exterior: Adobe Stock © alter_photo ©Lars Johansson

Interior Formatting: BB Formatting Adobe Stock © 213120122

Edited by Valorie Clifton

DEDICATION

To my readers, friends, and family. Thank you for embracing my dreams.

Chapter One

Amy

My job in life was to stay hidden and unnoticed, which suited me perfectly. Okay, that wasn't exactly my job, but it was an important part of being a nanny. The families I'd worked for loved having me a part of their world as long as I wasn't a part of *their* world. But I was okay with it. I knew my place, and I liked getting to tag along to exotic locales and experience worlds I'd never get to see except between the pages of a book. Plus, I absolutely loved children.

The one exception to being unseen and unheard was when I got to work with Daisy and Hunter. Tate, the little guy I nannied for, was nearly eight months old and Hunter's son. He was the best baby boy to watch, and Daisy, Hunter, and Tate were the perfect family unit. Watching them all together made my heart melt, but most of all, they made me feel like I was part of their magic.

And that family unit was what led me to Buttercup Lake in Wisconsin. My twin sister liked to call it the middle of nowhere, but I had the very distinct feeling that I was indeed somewhere… somewhere very special.

Daisy was actually Tate's soon-to-be stepmom if all things went according to Hunter's plan. And Tate's biological mom, Brielle, was married to an extremely wealthy man named Nick. Those two were how I initially got hired to watch little Tate in Chicago. It wasn't until Brielle decided to enlighten Hunter that he was Tate's father that I moved to Buttercup Lake a few months ago.

The whole thing happened so quickly that my head spun, and I was still trying to catch up. One minute, I was in a group of three nannies living in Chicago, and the next, I was spending the holidays in a small town in Wisconsin without my sister.

Thankfully, Daisy and Hunter welcomed me with open arms and showed me around a bit. They were completely different from Tate's biological mom. Brielle would rather I lurked in the shadows until I was needed. Funny enough, when I was with Brielle, I was needed a lot, and ironically, Daisy and Hunter only asked for help on rare occasions.

I stretched my toes in front of me and let out a happy sigh as I stared at the frozen lake through the floor-to-ceiling windows. Little fishing huts peppered the solid mass of ice and made me shiver just looking at them.

Brielle and Nick bought a home across the street from Hunter to make sharing custody easier for everyone, and their home was magnificent, with a beautiful view of the water, or so I was told. The lake had been frozen solid the moment I arrived in town.

I let out a happy hum and turned on the stereo as I stood and went to my bedroom. It was larger than any bedroom I'd ever had and even had a connecting ensuite. I'd managed to make it as much mine as possible. I'd painted the walls a soothing light blue, almost a grey color, and I'd hung a few black and white family photos on the wall of my sister from when we were young. I bought several African violets that I'd put in front of the window on a small, wrought-iron table that I'd picked up at a thrift store. If Brielle knew that part, she'd probably fall over. But I always loved searching for treasures, and this table qualified.

It gave me an escape and reminded me that tattered things could be loved again, kind of like me. Or at least I hoped I had a shot again.

I flipped on the lights and smiled at my little piece of

heaven. My sister was coming to visit, and I couldn't wait to show her around Buttercup Lake. It was so different from our version of the small town we'd both escaped.

Truth be told, I wasn't used to the kind of wealth that surrounded me, so maybe it would be different if I weren't encircled by these things. Although, they didn't bring the warmth that I imagined they would. It was definitely the town, not the things.

But I was grateful for the stereo system that piped through the entire home, or the house would settle into eerie silence since Brielle and Nick took Tate with them to fly out to Arizona for two weeks.

I'd offered to go with them, but they took the nanny who lived with them when they were in Chicago since she had family in Arizona.

Brielle and Nick found themselves jetting off to places all over the world, and I used to enjoy that perk of the job until I landed in Buttercup Lake.

I glanced out the window at the frozen lake and then back at my empty bed piled high with pillows and a white goose-down comforter. The thought of taking a warm bath and climbing underneath the covers on a Monday afternoon sounded incredible. It had been a long time since I'd had any time to myself, and tonight, I had a date with the local book club. The Sunshine Breakfast Club had been a quick way to meet some local people, and so far, they'd all been extremely sweet.

I pulled my sweater over my head and tossed it in the laundry basket before unfastening my bra and kicking off my jeans to land on top of the sweater.

"Nice work, Amy." I walked into the large bathroom covered in Carrera marble, turned on the water for the claw-foot tub, and dumped a ton of strawberry bubble bath under the faucet. It was hard to believe they went to this much expense in one of the guest rooms, but I certainly wasn't complaining.

I yawned, stretched to the ceiling, and wandered back into the bedroom to grab a pair of pajamas out of the armoire by the window. As I slid open the top drawer, something caught my eye outside the window. I pulled out a flannel pair of pajamas and craned my neck, looking out the glass. Whatever it was, it had been dark and fast, maybe a bald eagle swooping down to get the night's dinner. Things like that weren't completely unheard of when you lived near water in Wisconsin.

I tilted my head, scanning the yard leading to the lake, and saw absolutely nothing. I let out a little hum to the music that played as I turned around and smiled at the thought of a bubble bath.

But then… out of the corner of my eye, I saw a man.

Not an eagle. A man!

A large boulder of a man.

My hands flailed into the air, the pajamas went flying, and I screamed at the top of my lungs as I dove to the floor, my legs skittering and peeling out in all directions as terror thumped through me as I searched for the jammies I threw in the air.

The sound of my squeals caught the man's attention as he turned around to look through the glass. His hand flew to his brow ridge as he squinted through the window.

To my horror, Sheriff Nate stood right outside my bedroom, peering into the house.

Nate hadn't even been pointed in my direction until I screamed, and now he was staring right in my vicinity.

Why did I scream? I should have known there wouldn't be any bad guys around here. It was too cold for peeping Toms.

It didn't help that I'd had a silly crush on this glorious mound of a man, and now he stared through the glass, searching for the source of the ruckus.

But it was me.

I was the naked ruckus, sliding along the floor like a

nearly paralyzed earthworm, heading for my flannels.

This was what my life had come to in the middle of Wisconsin. I wiggled around the floor like a naked earthworm, praying the sheriff didn't turn and look inside the window. But he did... because that's just my luck.

Right when my fingers clutched the pink flannel top, Nate's eyes connected with mine. His mouth opened and shut as his eyes fell to my bare breasts before shifting right back up to my gaze.

I apparently hadn't been quick enough to cover myself. My pulse pounded so hard I could feel it between my ears like a ping-pong ball.

The entire town was going to hear about this. I just knew it.

Welcome to Buttercup Lake, Amy, boobs and all.

Nate spun around and walked away from the window and around the house as I jumped up, pulled the shirt over my head, and pushed my legs through the flannel pants.

To say I was mortified didn't even begin to take in all the emotions rolling through me.

The doorbell rang, and I shook my head.

Great. Now we get to talk about it.

I entered the bathroom, turned off the bathwater, and went to the front door.

What in the world was the sheriff doing in my backyard, and did he really need to come to the front of the house?

I shook my head, groaned a little, and opened the door to see Nate, his dark hair looking disheveled as he removed his hat. The moment I'd met this man at a holiday party, my heart fluttered, so I did my best to stay away.

Far away.

Clearing my throat, I raised my brows and waited as he clutched his hat between his large hands.

His beautiful hazel eyes fastened on mine as he pressed his lips together and gave me a slight nod. The sheriff's rugged appeal dripped from his expression, and a brooding smirk lodged behind his gaze. I felt the familiar pool of giddiness and uncertainty swirl in my belly as I stared at the man in front of me. It had been so long since... No. I wasn't going to go there.

I cleared my throat so any squeak of embarrassment would be gone. "Sheriff McKay?"

"I apologize. I don't usually go poking around residents' yards, but I received a nuisance call about a missing mule down the road at Honey Leaf Lodge, and someone said they spotted the animal here. At any rate, I remember Nick telling me they were headed to Arizona, so I thought the place was empty."

"Nope."

"Well, I see that now, Amy. Or, I mean, I saw that. No, I didn't see anything." He shook his head and slid his hat on, and my brows arched even higher as I folded my arms over my chest. "What I'm saying is that in the future, I will ring the doorbell first."

My lips tugged at the sight of Nate McKay fumbling all over himself. He'd always struck me as an extremely confident man with zero vulnerabilities or weaknesses. But he seriously looked like if I even just blew in his direction, he'd crumple and fall to the ground.

It was a nice change.

"I wouldn't have answered, anyway," I assured him.

I'd always had this problem trait where I wanted to make everyone else feel comfortable around me, even if I were dying inside.

And I was most definitely dying. At best, he only saw my breasts. At worst, well… everything else.

Nate frowned. "What do you mean?"

"I'm from Chicago. We don't answer doors if we aren't expecting someone."

His hazel eyes stayed on mine, but he ground his strong jaw from side to side. His dark hair was barely visible under his hat. The day's stubble barely surfaced along the squareness of his chin, only highlighting his scrumptious lips that I shouldn't be noticing.

"Then maybe I could get your phone number so I could call next time."

Was he asking for my phone number, like, to ask me out?

I chuckled and nodded. "Are you flirting with one of your—"

"Amy, I promise you I'm not flirting. If I were, you'd have no shadow of a doubt." He smiled, and an electric shock pulsed through me. "I'm merely protecting us from this happening again."

"Protecting?"

He nodded. "Protecting."

"Good to know. My bubble bath is getting cold, which is why you saw me naked, so if you don't mind, I'd like to get back to it before all the bubbles pop."

"Absolutely." He gave a quick nod. "About that number, Amy?"

I held in a chuckle and recited my cellphone number as he wrote it down on his notepad.

And he didn't deny that he saw all of me earlier, which only made me want to slink under the couch behind me.

When I finished, his hazel eyes flicked back up to mine, and the look in his gaze nearly took my breath away.

Nate didn't say anything. He didn't have to for me to know what was happening inside.

Or was it only what I wanted to be happening inside?

I could feel the heat peppering my body as I drew a breath and glanced over his shoulder at his SUV.

"I'll let you know if I spot a mule gallivanting around the lake," I assured him, "But I need to get back to my bath."

"Please do," he said softly with a nod, touching the brim of his hat. "And I'm sorry about earlier. I really didn't see anything with the glare."

I wasn't sure that I believed him.

"Have a good afternoon, Sheriff."

Nate turned around and started down the walk. "But I appreciate you putting on some pajamas before you answered, or I wouldn't be able to remember why I was here, Amy."

A little yelp rolled off my lips as I shut the door and rested my forehead on the wood. The way he constantly said my name made my heart beat a little faster than it should. And it's not like he was doing it because he *liked* me. It was his job. Probably some tactic to soothe the perps or victims.

Amy, this.

Amy, that.

But I just loved hearing it roll off his tongue.

I was doomed.

I chuckled to myself and groaned.

Never mind that since I briefly met him, I couldn't stop thinking about him.

And then this.

Why could nothing in my life go normally? Why did there have to be these little reminders thrown at me that I wasn't meant for relationships, or really, any contact with the general population? I was just like a magnet for embarrassing situations. It's why I liked living in a big city like Chicago. I could dump a mocha down my shirt when I missed my mouth, and nobody would remember or care. Here, it might be on the front page of the paper.

I pushed myself off the door and slowly made my way to the bubbly tub, trying as hard as I could to push the only man to have seen me naked in the last decade out of my head.

But he wouldn't budge. Even as I slid into the warm water, the expression in his hazel eyes filled me with something I couldn't describe, and I was worried about why I wanted to know more.

Because the last time I'd cared, it nearly killed me.

Chapter Two

Nate

"For shit's sake," I grumbled to the receptionist.

Florence had been the face of the community center, police, and mayor's office for as long as I could remember. She didn't look a day over fifty, but rumor had it that she was nearing seventy. "Do you think there was even a mule loose?"

Florence's bright blue eyes fastened on mine, and she flashed me a coy grin. "The only way to find out is to call the March family over at Honey Leaf Lodge. What's got you so riled up, anyway?"

My scalp instantly heated as Amy's lush body flashed into my head. Before long, sweat would be running down my forehead just from the memory of her naked body rolling around like a convulsing earthworm.

Dang. I never thought that could be so sexy.

She was all curves and softness and…

I tugged on the brim of my cowboy hat and peered over her shoulder at the logbook. "What time did the first call come in?"

"Well, the first call came over the non-emergency line at noon saying a mule had been seen wandering around town," she informed me.

"By whom?"

Her dark brows rose. "Millie."

"Well, that right there is suspicious." I shook my head.

She ignored my comment and continued. "And then we got a call from someone saying a mule was missing from the petting zoo at the lodge."

"Who?"

She shook her head. "It was anonymous."

"Sure, it was." I folded my arms over my chest and stared at the logbook. "Why can't I ever read what you've written?"

"Shorthand," she replied. "And finally, Hunter called in that he saw a mule wandering around Brielle's home."

Hunter wouldn't be in on something like this, would he?

The guy had been as single as they came up until recently. But I'd gotten the distinct feeling that since the holidays, the Sunshine Breakfast Club had been trying to push Amy and me together, whether we wanted it or not.

Sure, the book club looked innocent from afar, but I knew what the ringleader was all about. Millie was incessantly trying to ram the idea of love down every living being within a ten-mile radius.

And I was suddenly feeling like the invite to the book club that night to discuss personal safety had been a sham. Flo was the one who'd suggested I accept, but now, I didn't know whom to trust.

But after this afternoon's events, I had the distinct feeling that this was a love connection gone awry.

"Thanks for the information. I'll give the Honey Leaf Lodge a shout." I chewed on my bottom lip as I made my way to my office.

The term *office* was generous.

It was more like a shoebox for elves. My predecessor, who also happened to be my uncle, didn't think we even needed an office for the sheriff because he felt the sheriff should be out with the town ninety-nine percent of the time. But that was before computers became such an integral part of our lives... say, decades ago, and he didn't believe there was a need for a desk, let alone shelves and extra chairs. Nowadays, it felt like eighty percent of my job had to do with pushing papers and filing reports online.

I kicked out my chair, which rolled into the wall with a thud. I sat down with a bang to the wall again and sighed.

A jacket I'd lost over a month ago fell from a shelf. I stood and picked it up. "What? That doesn't make sense," I muttered to myself.

I would have seen it there, and I would never put my stuff on the shelf. It was too dusty. I turned and looked around my office, feeling like maybe it wasn't just me calling it home. I reached up and touched my cowboy hat. I was still breaking this one in because my old one went missing, too.

Oddly.

Whatever. I didn't have time to think about these things. I took a seat again and rubbed my temples.

Today had been a day, and the headache wrapping its tentacles around every single brain cell I had left was brutal.

There were so many issues that went along with seeing Amy's naked body writhing around in her own bedroom. First of all, it was in her own bedroom. What was I doing looking inside?

Well, I knew that. It sounded like a dolphin was getting stabbed to death, and it was my job to make sure that if someone needed help, they'd get help.

Me?

I was the help.

I'd also turned into the town's peeping Tom… so that was great.

As the computer sprang to life, I stared at the empty form where I usually filled in the blanks without even a thought. But I suddenly didn't know what to say or how to say it.

After all, it wasn't every day that I happened to see a woman I had a mild crush on… naked.

And whatever I put in here was public record.

But first things first. I picked up our ancient brown phone and dialed the number for the Honey Leaf Lodge.

A friendly woman answered. "Honey Leaf. How may I help you?"

"Hey, this is Sheriff Nate. Did you, by any chance, lose a mule?"

She sucked in a deep breath and groaned. "Oh, no. Did Betty Boop get out again?"

"Well, I don't know. That's what I was hoping to find out."

"She is a stinker, that one, but she doesn't usually leave the property. Hold on a sec. I'll check with my brother."

She covered the phone and hollered, "Hey, Liam. Did our escape artist get out again? The sheriff is on the phone."

A few seconds went by as some muffled discussion went on. "Nope. Betty is where she's supposed to be."

My stomach turned. It had been a setup.

"Okay. Great. Must be someone else's mule," I informed her. "And who is this?"

"Fifi, or I mean Fiona March. Sorry. You probably want my legal name. It's Fiona."

I chuckled. "Nah, you're fine."

"Is there anything else I can help you with, sheriff?"

I shoved my fingers through my hair and chuckled to myself. "No, that tells me everything. Thanks for your time, Fiona."

Hanging up the phone, I took a deep breath and shook my head. *If the Sunshine Breakfast Club wants to have a little fun with me, maybe I'll have to have some fun with them.*

I'd be the dutiful sheriff who talked about self-defense at tonight's meeting, but there would come a time when I'd flop this whole matchmaking book club on its head and teach Millie a lesson. I couldn't be chasing imaginary mules around town. It was a waste of taxpayers' money.

In the meantime, I needed to determine what to include in this report and what to leave out.

I should call Amy and let her know what details I needed to add to the report. I scratched the scruff on my chin and chuckled. Nah. That wasn't a great idea. It was hard enough getting Amy out of my head. I didn't need her sexy voice drilling through my thoughts as well.

The truth was that Amy had intrigued me from the first time I'd met her. Hunter had invited me to a holiday party she'd attended, but I'd actually met her at the coffee shop a few days prior. I wasn't in uniform, so she probably didn't remember.

But I certainly did.

Every single thing about her had been a turn-on, and quite frankly, it had been annoying.

"Ugh," I groaned, smoothing my palms over my face. "Get a hold of yourself, Nate."

A little giggle erupted near my door. I dropped my hands from my face to see Florence holding her purse.

"Anything else you need before I head out early?"

Early?

"Remember, I had an appointment at four?" she reminded me.

I smiled. "Oh, right. I'll see you tomorrow."

She tilted her head, frowning. "Don't get so worked up over the mule. It's not your first escaped mule and won't be your last. Just be glad it's not one of Frank's bulls down the road. You'll find that mule."

I laughed, spinning slightly in my chair as I stretched my legs under the desk. "Good point."

Florence wandered out of the hallway, and I couldn't help but smile. I'd often wondered whether I wanted to leave this small town for something bigger, a place with more action.

Between roosters waking up neighbors in unauthorized zones, chasing down imaginary mules, and pulling over farm equipment during unlawful hours, it wasn't exactly the type of work that used my detective skills.

Yet, I still wasn't sure whether that bothered me.

I stared at the computer screen and let out a deep breath.

Just as I reached for the phone, a woman cleared her throat at my door.

The energy in the room immediately shifted. It was like electricity zipped through my body at an unstoppable rate.

I slowly brought my gaze to meet the woman standing at the door holding a small cardboard box of something I couldn't see from my vantage point.

"Sorry to bother you, Sheriff," Amy said, inhaling a deep breath. She nipped her bottom lip and shifted her weight from one foot to the other.

I tried to ignore how cute she looked fully clothed.

"You're not a bother at all, Amy." And I meant it. "How can I help you? Did you find the mule?"

A smile touched her lips, and her shoulders relaxed. "Sorry, no equine sightings."

She licked her lips nervously, which, for some reason, was an extreme turn-on. I glanced at the blank form on my screen and nodded.

"But I did bring you some red velvet cupcakes to kind of wipe away anything you might have seen from earlier." She smiled brighter and raised her brows, shoving the box to me. "Millie said they're amazing."

Those *were* my favorite cupcakes, but I wasn't sure why the ringleader of the local book club knew or cared. "Wipe away what, in particular?"

Her brows rose, and her light brown eyes sparkled. "You know. What you saw… It's a small town. I want to make a good impression. I don't know how long I'll be working here, but I want to make it as uneventful as possible." She took a few steps into my tiny office, and the sweet smells of vanilla and cupcakes swirled around me. "Earlier, when I was trying to relax in the bath, the sudden thought popped into my head that you'd probably need to write a report on the call and…"

She set the cupcakes down on my desk and leaned over the small box. Her eyes connected with mine, and it took everything I had to keep my eyes on hers.

"Are you bribing an officer, Amy?" My lips curled slightly.

"I just might be, Sheriff Nate." Her eyes stayed on mine, and the electricity zipped between us.

The heat running through me was nearly unbearable. I ripped my gaze away and looked back at the computer screen.

"It's funny you dropped in now. I was about to fill out the report."

Her hands moved to the small box. She slowly started to unfasten the flap. "I'm sure you're starving, Sheriff. I know I am."

My gaze flicked to hers, and her smile stayed locked in place as she sat in the chair next to my desk. I reached for a cup of stale coffee and let out a slow breath.

What was it about this woman?

"I'll just stay here while you write up your information. You know, in case you have any questions." She tilted her head ever so slightly as her gaze dropped to the open box and she gasped.

I looked down and nearly spat out the coffee when I

saw the two cupcakes side by side. Peach frosting with a pink nipple on each… err, I mean a dollop of pink icing on the top of each.

Her jaw dropped down as a gasp slithered from her lips.

She quickly flipped the lid closed. "What kind of bakery did Millie send me to? I didn't know you had a naughty bakery here. It's a small town in the middle of nowhere."

I snickered and shook my head, watching the rosiness slowly roll up Amy's neck to land squarely on her cheeks. "We aren't nowhere, for your information. We're very much somewhere. And I don't know what you're talking about. The cupcakes looked perfectly decent."

Amy shifted uncomfortably in her seat, and I couldn't stop looking at her as embarrassment thrummed through her. She tucked some dark golden-brown hair behind her ear and brought her soft brown eyes to mine.

There was no doubt about it. Those cupcakes looked like a pair of breasts, possibly Amy's.

I clenched my eyes shut and shook my head. No. I couldn't go there. I just kept in my laughter and turned back to Amy.

"You said Millie was involved?" I typed Nick's address into the computer.

Amy was staring at the box.

"Well, she didn't make the cupcakes." She slowly lifted the lid again as if the cupcakes were about to leap out at her. "She just ordered them for me."

Her eyes connected with mine, and I spotted the rosiness in her cheeks.

There was absolutely zero doubt that someone had thought it would be funny to make naughty cupcakes. It's just unfortunate that it happened on the day I actually saw Amy's breasts.

"They look like perfectly fine cupcakes to me," I said, trying to keep in my laughter. There was absolutely no way I'd agree with Amy about what these cupcakes actually looked like, not today.

Her mouth dropped open as her jaw ticked slightly. "I… My…" She scowled at the cupcakes. "You can't tell me those don't look like two boo—" She stopped herself.

I chuckled and reached for a cupcake.

"I'm sure it's just on top of mind since… you know… everything happened earlier."

"I thought you said you didn't see anything."

I winked. "And I stand by that. Red velvet, you said?"

She nodded, and her lips perked into a wide smile. "You're very hard to read, Sheriff."

Amy grabbed a cupcake and took a bite, letting out a little moan. The sound nearly drove me over the edge as her eyes closed and the frosting melted from her lips.

"I thought those were for me," I said, chuckling.

"One for you and one for me." She held half a cupcake in her hand and grinned. There was a little bit of frosting left on her lip that I was tempted to wipe away, but I knew better. Just wishful thinking. "This way, it just looks like a cupcake."

"They always just looked like cupcakes, Amy." I laughed and reached for the remaining red velvet cupcake.

She chuckled. "You're good at lying. That concerns me."

I took a bite. Amazing, like always. "It shouldn't."

"So, will the town of Buttercup Lake know that the sheriff saw me naked?" she asked, licking her lip. I tore my gaze away right when I heard a rustle outside my office.

My eyes landed on Flo, who was outside my office with a smirk on her face as she eyed Amy and me.

"Don't mind me. I'm just retracing my steps to find my car keys." Her brows moved up and down as Amy froze in her chair, not turning to see the receptionist.

"Well, your secret is safe with me," I assured Amy, looking over Amy's shoulder. "But I can't promise secrecy from anyone else."

"Oh, here they are. Right in my pocket." Flo hummed as she turned around and started down the hallway. "See you tomorrow, Sheriff."

"See you tomorrow, Flo." I clicked my mouse, brought the screen to life, and started typing. "So, I just put in that I heard a ruckus from inside Nick and Brielle's home and looked through the window to see the nanny…" I glanced at Amy.

"To see the nanny getting ready for a bath."

My brow arched. "In this town, that will lead to questions."

She nodded and leaned across the desk, propping herself on her elbows. "How about getting clothes out of the drawer and singing to the music playing? It's not a lie. I was doing that before I saw a huge hulk of a man standing outside my window. And I am a completely open book. So, I'd rather have a lot of details added or I'll wind up telling people anyway."

I chuckled, noticing the vanilla scent intensified the closer Amy got, and it was nearly intoxicating. "Hulk of a man?"

She scowled and folded her arms over her chest and looked a little embarrassed. "Like you don't know you are."

I smiled and shook my head. "Listen, I'll just say that I searched the premises, ran into you, and never found the missing donkey."

Her lips pursed in confusion. "I thought it was a mule."

My brows rose in surprise. "You know the difference?"

She laughed, and the sound was like euphoria surrounding me. "Of course, I know the difference between a donkey and a mule." Amy let out a relieved sigh and nodded. "Sounds like a great summary. Now, if you don't mind, I'm off to the book club."

My eyes widened. "You're part of the Sunshine Breakfast Club?"

Amy nodded with a slight dimple surfacing on her right cheek. "It seemed like the best way to make friends here. Why? Is there a problem with that, Sheriff?"

I folded my hands and let out a chuckle. "No problem at all, Amy."

Her eyes connected with mine, and I felt a charge of something I hadn't felt in forever.

Chapter Three

Amy

The howling wind scraped my cheeks as I climbed out of my car and trudged toward the community center where the book club met. The meeting had originally been scheduled for tomorrow morning, but a weather alert had been issued for a blizzard to arrive tonight.

Judging by the wicked breeze, it decided to come early. I hauled a jug of apple cider and my book to the door as I attempted to knee it open just as another gust of wind slammed it shut.

Grumbling under my breath, I set the jug down and pulled hard on the door. My rear kept it propped open as I reached for the jug.

The smell of garlic swept through the air as I heard

ladies laughing down the hall. Tonight's potluck was going to be a good one.

The door banged behind me, and I glanced around the community center that had been decorated for St. Patrick's Day even though we hadn't made it out of February. Little green shamrocks hung over the doorways leading into the various meeting rooms, and an oversized stuffed leprechaun sat happily in the corner with gift tags hanging off it to provide needs for different families.

It was little things like the giving tree, or in this instance, the leprechaun, that reminded me of how sweet it could be to live in a small town. Buttercup Lake was very different from the small town my sister and I grew up in. I wanted to believe where we'd grown up had changed, but I'd been back enough times to know it was stuck in a time capsule of despair. The haves had plenty, and the have-nots had even less.

"Amy, thank goodness." Millie clapped her hands and skipped a little as she headed my way. "We're not in our usual room, but I'm so glad you came with this juice. Cammie was supposed to bring pop, but her whole crew is down with the flu."

Many referred to Millie as the matchmaking queen of Buttercup Lake, but I hadn't seen any evidence of that. She was just a sweet older lady who enjoyed good books and getting the community together. She was a recent widow, but she'd managed to pair up with a good friend of hers. I'd see them around town from time to time, and they were super cute.

I thought about how easy it was for some people like Millie to find love. I definitely wasn't one of those women. For some reason, I liked to zero in on completely emotionally unavailable men, and if they happened to be narcissists—even better!

That's what worried me about the sheriff. I actually thought he was super cute and charismatic.

Charming, actually.

So, he probably just hid his ego problems better than the rest I'd fallen for, regardless of what Hunter and Daisy had hinted.

But with all of my dating disasters, I finally realized it was me.

I was the issue.

My picker was off, and I didn't think there was much help for changing that. My sister always loved to tell me as much, too. I secretly couldn't wait until she arrived tomorrow so I could get her take on Nate.

She'd been there with me through some serious jerks,

and she'd also been there for me when everything in my life went sideways with Leo. He and I had been best friends growing up, and I'd always felt safe with him, and then…

Life did its usual number and made me doubt everything I knew about friendship, love, and hope.

The betrayal still sat at the surface of my heart if I thought about it too much, so I never did.

I learned a lot, and I moved on.

And away.

But none of my previous dating traumas mattered because Nate seemed about as interested in me as a sack of potatoes rotting in a corner of a grocery store.

"Grace brought some amazing meatballs, and Flo picked up some brownies from her sister. They are amazing." Millie's bright gaze anchored on mine. "Anyone who says you can't have dessert before dinner isn't trustworthy, by the way."

I chuckled and nodded, following Millie into the room. "Agreed."

"Speaking of sweets, how did the sheriff like his cupcakes?"

My cheeks turned fire-engine red as I thought about the two cupcakes that resembled me this afternoon. "Uh, well. I ate one of them, and they were great."

"Aw, what a sweet guy that Nate is. He's always the type to share." Millie nodded.

I grinned. "He didn't share, exactly. I just grabbed one."

Millie giggled as we walked over to the buffet table. "That's my girl. Just reach out and grab what you need in life. If it's a cupcake, then by golly, get it."

My grin widened as I found a spot to put the jug of cider when my eyes skipped to a platter of cupcakes.

The same cupcakes from earlier.

But they looked anything but obscene. They were just… peach and pink cupcakes.

Mortification slowly spread through me at the thought of the sheriff. No wonder he didn't know what I was talking about. They didn't look like breasts. They didn't look like *my* breasts. They looked like springy cupcakes.

"You look like you saw a ghost," Millie said, clutching my wrist. "Are you okay?"

I shook my head and laughed. "Yeah. Just one of those days."

"Hey, Amy." I recognized Daisy's sing-song voice behind me and spun around, thankful for the distraction. She dashed over and gave me a squeeze. "Did Hunter text you yet about Tate?"

My heart dropped. "Is everything okay with Tate?"

She rubbed my arm and nodded. "Oh, yes. The little doll is doing just great in Arizona, but we've got exciting news."

I cocked my head. "Yeah?"

Her eyes widened, as did her grin. "Nick has to go to Japan for four months."

My stomach dipped. The thought of going somewhere so far away for four months sounded horrible. I was just finally getting grounded here in Buttercup Lake. My sister was even coming for a visit.

"Anyway, Brielle agrees that it would be too hard on Tate to go back and forth, so we get to have him for four months. It's easier for her to fly in for a week or two than to pack up Tate, the nannies, you know the drill." Daisy shrugged and glanced around the room. "Personally, I don't know how she can leave him at all. But four months?"

I knew what Daisy was thinking. She never had to say it, and no one did. But Brielle was unique, and her parenting style wasn't for everyone. The truth was that Hunter, Daisy, and little Tate benefited from Brielle's choices. Tate would grow up being the most loved little boy in the world, and especially in Buttercup Lake.

Daisy reached for a paper plate. "So, what this really

means is that you're going to have a wonderful vacation for the next few months getting to know the town here."

I chuckled. "Yeah?"

"I'd be surprised if we'll need much help. Hunter's focused on opening the bar this summer, but he's mostly overseeing contractors at this point. He's looking forward to spending so much time with his son, and so am I."

"I bet you are." I nodded, seeing the love wash through Daisy's gaze.

"Anyway, that's the big update." She put a spoonful of meatballs on her plate and reached for a slice of cheesy bread. "Did you hear about that escaped mule today?"

I froze. Had word gotten around that fast?

"Uh, yeah. The sheriff came by Nick and Brielle's house looking for it."

Millie raised her hand and waved at someone behind Daisy. Millie threw us a smile and rushed over to whomever she'd spotted.

"Oh, yeah? Why's that?" Daisy's brows rose.

"I guess someone reported a sighting."

Daisy chuckled and furrowed her brows. "Is that so?"

I tucked my book under my arm and reached for a plate as Maya and Grace wandered over. They were sisters who also happened to be Millie's granddaughters.

"What did you think of the first few chapters?" Maya asked as I scooped some potato salad onto my plate.

"The sheriff is absolutely lovable. I certainly hope Claire goes for him."

Maya nodded in agreement. "Yeah. A complete hulk of a man with a heart of gold."

"It's too bad men like that don't exist in real life," I muttered, putting a chive roll next to the potato salad.

Daisy gasped. "They do, Amy."

Maya grinned. "It's true. Cash is an absolute dream, and believe me, I'd kissed a lot of warty toads before him."

I laughed, shaking my head. "I'll keep that in mind. For now, reading about heroes between the pages is more fun. I've had my fill of real men. I honestly don't think my heart or mind can take any more tries."

Grace and Maya chuckled as Daisy looked at me with a sympathetic expression.

"Okay, everyone. Let's gather around and talk about our sweet waitress and schmexy sheriff." Millie eyed the group before her gaze landed on me. "Why don't you sit next to me, Amy?"

I shrugged. "Sure." Turning to Daisy, I laughed and lowered my voice. "Did she just call the book boyfriend for this month *schmexy*?"

Daisy grinned and balanced her plate with a drink. "I hope I'm even half as with it at her age."

I made my way over to the empty chair next to Millie and sat down, placing the plate of food on my lap as I moved the book from under my arm.

"Okay, Ladies." Millie glanced around the room and then her eyes locked on me. I quickly stared down at my plate of food and nibbled some cheesy bread. "Who thinks that Claire's ex is going to follow her to Fireweed Island?"

I raised my hand, along with all the other women.

"Me too. I'm thinking that we've got some build-up, and then *bam*. The sheriff will save the day." A dopy expression traced Millie's face. "I think it would be incredible to date a sheriff."

Grace laughed. "You'd better not tell Carter."

"Oh, he knows that my fantasy of dating a sheriff is impossible. I don't think a police officer in his mid-eighties even exists." She chuckled and then unexpectedly turned her whole body toward me. "What about you, Amy? Would you date a man of the law?"

I choked on my cheesy bread, and Millie slapped my back as my eyes watered. "Umm. Yeah? I suppose I'd date anyone with any type of job. It would be a huge step up."

"Ah, that's good. You don't want to discriminate and

accidentally eliminate." She waggled her white brows. "Right, Ladies?"

The group of about twenty women chuckled, nodding.

The door creaked open, and I glanced up to see Sheriff Nate, dressed in his uniform, march into the room, and it was like all the air had immediately sucked out of my lungs before one last flutter in my chest allowed me to breathe again.

He looked extremely gorgeous, commanding... mysterious.

But I got the distinct feeling that he didn't exactly want to be here.

"Okay, Ladies. On that note, let's read six chapters for next week's meeting." She stood and smiled at the sheriff. "Now, the sheriff is here to talk to us about things to watch out for."

Nate's rumbly laugh rolled through the room, and his eyes landed on me. I dropped my head quickly and glanced down at my plate of food. I didn't know what it was about this guy that made me feel...

Unhinged?

Confused?

Delirious?

I drew a deep breath and stuck a scoop of potato salad

in my mouth, but I got the distinct feeling that the sheriff was watching me. I lifted my head to see Nate's eyes locked on me, and heat swirled through me as I instinctively licked the potato salad off my lips before dabbing it with a napkin.

I mean, you couldn't get sexier than that, right?

A knowing smirk surfaced across Nate's expression as a shot of electricity ran through me, just like in his office.

Or was I making it up?

He barely gave me the time of day most of the time.

Maybe there was no smirk or smoldering look in his gaze.

I dragged my gaze back to the potato salad and sulked a little.

"I think it's safe to say that we live in a pretty safe town, but I'm here to tell you that it's never a bad idea to stay situationally aware," he started.

Millie nodded, pulling Nate toward the middle of the room. He stood tall and glanced around the room, running his hand through his hair and shaking his head as his eyes landed on me again.

Without warning, Millie snapped her fingers at me and pointed at Nate. "How about Amy is our model for you to use?"

"It's not like I'm teaching Karate or something,

Millie. I wasn't thinking I needed a—"

Once again, he didn't want to be physically near me. So it had to have been my crazy imagination.

I shook my head. "Yeah, Millie. My belly is a little full of everything I've eaten."

Not sexy at all. Next, maybe I can enlighten him about indigestion.

Millie narrowed her eyes on me. "Hogwash. Didn't you say you'd date a sheriff? Might as well give one a spin tonight."

My mouth dropped open, and a gasp rolled off my lips. "That's not exactly what—"

A fuzzy static echoed through the room as Nate dropped his gaze to his belt, pulling his transceiver from its holder.

"*Sheriff, we might need some assistance. I think we found your rogue donkey. She's in a bit of a pickle. She's got… Well, you'd have to see it to believe it. Emergency crew is on the way.*"

"Mule," I corrected, and all the women glanced at me.

"I'll be right there," Nate answered into his handheld transceiver before he looked around the room, but when his gaze landed on me, my pulse soared. "I'm sorry, Ladies. I'll have to reschedule." He didn't take his eyes off me, and it felt... crazy.

I had to be imagining things, but I swore that there was some weird electricity zipping between us. When I thought I might implode from looking into his eyes, he spun on his heels and started toward the door.

"Just remember to stay vigilant. Don't get complacent. And for crying out loud, lock your front doors and close your blinds." He glanced over his shoulder and smiled...

At me.

I was sure of it.

Chapter Four

Nate

Maybe I was getting a little paranoid about the Sunshine Breakfast Club.

But I'd heard stories. I'd seen their handiwork.

Shoot, I'd been tapped once or twice myself to bring two unsuspecting souls together in the name of love, and it was all fine.

Fine until they wanted to involve me.

I scratched my chin and glanced at the photographs from the night before as I sat in my kitchen, drinking some coffee before my day at the office started.

We still hadn't tracked down the mule's rightful owner, so he was currently in the garage in my backyard about to be driven to my parents' farm, Cherry Hill Orchards. I wouldn't normally keep a mule in my garage, but it was twenty below with the windchill last night.

Thankfully, my parents had a cherry orchard, mostly for U-pickers, but they also had a few farm animals, mainly to keep my mom happy. It was also on the backside of my property. It just so happened our driveways were on opposite county roads. I moved into the original old farmhouse with an extensive wraparound porch that I managed to hang flowers from in the summer without killing them.

The porch swing was left over from when my parents owned the place, and I'd added a few rocking chairs for nights I spent with the guys, shooting the breeze, drinking some beer, and watching fireflies. I'd always been fond of this place, so when my parents wanted to sell it after building their own home on the backside, I was fortunate enough to be able to snatch it.

I still didn't have a clue about the mule's origin. Usually, if we found an animal around here, we also found the farmer or rancher who'd lost it.

And after the shenanigans from last night, maybe the owners were downright exhausted with the mule.

I'd never seen anything like it, really, and I didn't even know a mule could stretch like it had. But when I'd pulled up last night right before the blizzard set in, I spotted the mule wedged between a piece of lake ice and a canoe, except that its front hooves seemed to be securely in the boat. It was as if this mule thought he was going to hang out in the canoe on the frozen lake.

The mule was actually lucky to even be here with the storm hitting like it did last night. Probably an hour more, and it would have been a goner.

And then there was Amy.

When I entered the room last night, her bright eyes watched me, and I was almost certain she was happy to see me—except I was sure she was even happier when I left.

It didn't matter, anyway. I wasn't the relationship type and thought the Sunshine Breakfast Club knew that.

There was just too much at stake in a one-on-one relationship. I wasn't ready for it, and I never would be. The thought of falling for someone I couldn't adequately care for was enough to stop me in my tracks.

I'd already lost someone I'd cared about once, and I knew I couldn't go through that again.

A double honk sounded out front, and I stood from the chair, polished off the last cup of coffee, and made my way to the front door to see my dad with his horse trailer hooked up behind his orange pickup.

It wasn't exactly the best time to drive around with a

horse trailer, but our crews did a decent job maintaining most of the roadways. Paul, the guy I'd hired to plow my drive, had been here before the sun had even cracked the horizon.

I pulled on my coat and stepped onto my porch. The steps and walkway were pretty clear from the salt I'd dumped onto it earlier after I'd shoveled. It wasn't exactly easy living in the Northwoods this time of year, but I couldn't imagine being anywhere else.

My dad climbed out of his truck and gave a quick wave before opening the trailer up. He walked over and tugged on the knit cap my mom had made for him. She made them for everyone she came into contact with. If you were family, you had at least ten or twenty caps stuffed on a shelf in the closet.

"So, where's the crazy beast?" my dad asked, laughing. He had a harness and lead with him.

I chuckled and shook my head. "I didn't really trust her not to either freeze to death or take off again, so I have her in my workshop-slash-garage."

My dad grimaced. "That's gonna be messy."

I laughed and shook my head. "The mule and I had an understanding. I saved her life, so she wasn't going to make my life hard this morning."

The truth was that I'd thrown in some hay in the back

of my workshop, which was a four-car garage on the backside of my property, and hoped for the best. Hopefully, it wouldn't be on the cement if she had some business to do.

As we trudged through the snow around the house, I glanced at my dad, who seemed to be slowing down a little more than usual.

"Everything okay?"

"Yeah. Just threw out my back the other night." He shrugged, waving me ahead.

"What were you doing?" I asked, unlocking the door.

"No comment," my dad muttered.

I threw my dad a strange look as I opened the door, and he grunted. "Fine. I was tying my snow boot. And I heard a click."

I chuckled. "That's too bad."

"I swear. The moment I hit sixty-three, it was like every joint in my body froze up on me." He shook his head as I closed the door behind him. "Getting old is a privilege. At least, that's what I tell myself every day. And then I see a woman like Millie roaming around town looking like she's ready to teach an aerobics class, and she's twenty years my senior, and I wonder what the hell I did wrong."

It was true. Millie was not only a fixture of Buttercup Lake. She'd unknowingly set an example for the community on how to age gracefully. She had spunk, fire, and a kind heart. All things which made me overlook her role in her incognito matchmaking club.

"Speaking of her, I have a feeling she might be trying to hook me up."

My dad looked surprised. "With whom?"

"No comment."

"Ah, you can tell your old man. I know better than to think they can pull anything off with you."

I laughed and clapped my dad's shoulder. "I don't know whether I should be offended or relieved?"

My dad chuckled. He was one of the toughest men I knew, both mentally and physically. In fact, he was kind of the black sheep of the family when he stood up to his father and explained that he didn't, in fact, want to go into law enforcement. His brother did, and he was my uncle who'd retired as the local sheriff here, but my dad didn't want anything to do with it.

There was always a part of me that wondered if I'd let my dad down a little bit by following in my uncle's footsteps instead of his own.

A braying noise erupted from the far corner where I'd stacked several large plastic totes, about shoulder height, to act as a wall. Truthfully, the mule could have just knocked them over, but I felt a kinship with her since I'd saved her from becoming an icicle.

The braying turned to a whinnying as her salt and pepper head nodded in our direction.

"Did you see that girl smile at us?" my dad asked, laughing. "I'll be darned."

The mule's coat was thick for winter and a beautiful salt and pepper in color. I'd never seen coloring so pretty.

We walked over to her, and my dad laughed as he softly kicked a column of totes out of the way. "Good thing you're a cop and not a farmer."

I rolled my eyes and laughed as my fingers dug into the thick mane of the mule. Her big brown eyes stayed on us as my dad petted her neck and talked softly to her.

"We'll find your home again, baby doll," my dad whispered. "And if not, you'll love it at Cherry Hill."

I smiled as the mule nuzzled its nose into my dad's arm and then looked over at me. I helped my dad secure the harness and scanned the hay.

"What did I tell you, Dad? She and I had an agreement. Hay's as clean as when I put it in here last night."

I walked over to the garage door opener and pressed the button for the far garage bay door to slowly open. The sound didn't faze the mule as my dad slowly walked her over to the opening. Some snow spilled into the garage, and I took the lead from my dad.

"I'll take her to the trailer," I offered.

Since my dad didn't refuse, it told me everything I needed to know about his back. He really was in rough shape.

As the mule and I wandered through the snow, my mind drifted to Amy. I hoped she got home alright before the heavy snow started to come down.

Of course, she did. I was the sheriff. If she hadn't gotten home safely last night, I would have heard about it.

Damn.

I shouldn't let myself care.

As we wound around my house and to the trailer, I let out a low breath and walked the mule into her new transportation. Since it was a short ride and there was only her inside, I didn't tie her up, but I did give her extra chin scratches.

"This is a lot better than how you got home last night, isn't it? A little more civilized?"

The mule gave a neigh, and I chuckled, thinking back to us putting her in the SWAT team's van. It was the SWAT for the county, but they housed it in our town. What they didn't know wouldn't hurt them, but I did take some great pictures to chide them with come April Fool's Day because I was that immature.

"She good?" my dad asked. I nodded and gave her one last scratch.

"You be good," I told the mule and climbed out of the trailer before closing the gate. "Thanks again, Dad."

"No need to thank me. Your mother is absolutely thrilled."

"Good. This can be an early Mother's Day present if no one claims her."

My dad scowled. "Your mom or the mule?"

"You're going to get yourself into big trouble."

I gave my dad a quick hug, and he climbed into his truck as I walked back inside to get ready for my day.

The only problem was that I couldn't stop thinking about the woman I should be forgetting. It wasn't like she was here for the long haul, anyway. She was a nanny, following the family who'd hired her.

I closed the front door, and a shiver ran through me as the heat from inside attempted to penetrate through my jacket.

Right when I thought my morning was going smoothly, I heard chatter on the transceiver and made my way back into my kitchen.

Millie's down. Ambulance is on the way.

Copy that. ETA under three minutes.

My blood froze. My mind froze.

I reached for my transceiver but didn't know what to say. For the first time in years, I didn't know what to do.

The one thing I knew for sure was that our town needed Millie.

Absolutely nothing could happen to Millie Bailey.

Nothing.

I reached for my cowboy hat, which still irritated me. My uncle incorporated it into our uniform in the nineties, and it had been a thorn in my side since I'd joined the force. I cleared my throat and got a grip as I clicked my thumb on the microphone.

"Address?"

"Outside Buttercup Java."

The sirens blared in the background. Medics would be there in less than a minute. I grabbed my keys, fastened my belt on, and zipped up my jacket to make my way to the scene.

As I quickly jogged down the hall to the door leading to my small garage, I felt my pulse pounding.

Damn it, Millie. You got this.

I quickly made my way into the SUV, opened the garage door behind me, and pulled into my driveway as my dad was pulling onto the main county road to get back to his property. I didn't want to startle my dad with the siren, so I waited until I'd pulled out of my drive and started down the other direction before I flipped it on.

In what felt like hours but was truly only minutes, I pulled up next to the ambulance and saw Millie strapped to the gurney as the medics lifted her into the ambulance.

And my heart fell.

Chapter Five

Amy

My hands shook, and I couldn't catch a deep breath. Seeing Millie on the sidewalk in pain, legs out from underneath her, made my heart stop. I dashed to her as I called for emergency help.

Millie had always seemed invincible, and in that moment, she looked as scared as I felt.

And it brought me back to that night I'd found Leo... the helplessness, the chaos.

The hurt.

I snapped into my training and did everything the dispatcher told me to do, but it wasn't until she'd been driven away that I collapsed into a chair inside the coffee shop.

Just last night, she was ribbing me about blushing in

front of Nate. Oh, how I wanted her to be okay.

"How are you holding up?" Abby asked. She set a mocha in front of me and sat down in the chair across the table, slowly reaching to squeeze my hand. Abby owned the local coffee shop, and we'd become friends through my coffee addiction. "You were amazingly calm."

"I'm in shock. It wasn't like Millie slipped. She just... went down." I shook my head, feeling the knot tighten in my belly. "I hope she's going to be okay."

Abby nodded as the coffee shop door swung open and Nate's gaze landed on me.

Even in awful times, it was hard not to like the guy. He strode into the place like everything was under control, even in the middle of chaos. His broad shoulders filled out his uniform in ways I shouldn't be thinking about.

"Millie's already at the hospital," he said as Abby hopped out of the chair. "Something tells me she's going to be as good as new."

I swallowed down my worry and took a sip of the mocha.

"Your usual, Nate?" Abby asked.

"That'd be great." He tipped his hat, and I couldn't help but curl my lips into a smile.

"Are you a cowboy or something?"

He laughed and pointed at the empty chair. "Do you mind?"

My heart skipped a beat, and I shook my head.

"Our family might have just adopted a mule, so technically, it might be a yes." His eyes fastened on mine. "How are you holding up?"

I nodded, surprised he asked. I wasn't used to men asking how I felt about much. It all went back to the dating narcissists problem.

"I'm doing okay. Just in shock that she went down. Do her granddaughters know?"

He nodded and pointed over his shoulder toward Main Street. "Grace happened to be at the antique store early today. I ran over and told her what had happened."

"Poor gals. She is the glue that binds that family together—and the town, really."

Abby set his drink down in front of him, and he thanked her.

"You know, I wanted to apologize for the other day." He lowered his voice. "I was so shocked by the turn of events, I don't even know if I apologized."

I laughed, shaking my head. "Well, I was even more shocked, so I can't remember either. But apology accepted. You were merely doing your job."

"If I'd known you were home, I wouldn't have wandered around the yard. I honestly thought you'd gone with Nick and Brielle."

"Not a problem, Sheriff. Besides, it's not like you *saw* anything, right?" I teased.

A twinkle in his gaze made me chuckle as he glanced at the clock on the wall and stood, raising his coffee. "Have a good rest of your day, Amy. Thanks for being a Good Samaritan."

He turned around and went outside, stopping only long enough to glance at the area where Millie went down.

I couldn't help but wonder what scared him away. Obviously, he was on duty, but he probably could have stayed for an extra minute.

I glanced at Abby. "Is Nate always like that?"

"Like what?" She glanced outside.

I shrugged. "I don't know... flighty?"

Abby chuckled and shook her head. "No. Usually, he hangs around and chats far too long for us to get anything done, and if my husband is here, it's impossible. The accident with Millie probably shook him."

I nodded. "Makes sense."

But honestly, I'd felt it from him the first time I'd ever met him—even when I dropped off the cupcakes at his office or at the holiday party I'd attended at Christmas. There was just something that made him either squirm a little or beeline in the other direction around me.

"Are you interested in the sheriff?" Abby asked, bringing over a slice of coffee cake.

I sucked in a wheeze and shook my head.

"I was only teasing. He's married to his job. Everyone knows he's an eternal bachelor. This is on the house."

My heart unexpectedly fell over this news. It wasn't like I actually thought anything would or could come of running into Nate now and again, but it spoke volumes to my ability to fall for unavailable men.

It was a curse.

There was something in the universe—a magnet, possibly—that just pulled me in if a guy wasn't into a serious relationship.

Now, my twin sister had the exact opposite problem. She got into relationships, and she stayed in them far too long. And in that instance, it generally wasn't the guy's fault or her fault. Every move they made wasn't hinged on toxicity. I admired her for it. She'd always been extremely blunt, and that carried over into her romantic relationships too.

I took a bite of the coffee cake as the buttery crumbles hit my tongue. "Amazing, Abby."

"Thank you. I've been trying to bake more and more of my own breakfast items."

"This is incredible." I nodded, taking another bite. "You know, I make a pretty amazing cherry fritter."

"Cherry? Yum. I've only had apple."

"I'll bring some by sometime."

"I'd love it. You know, Nate's family owns a cherry orchard."

I straightened in my chair. "Seriously?"

"Yup. He lives on one side of the property, and his parents live on the other, where the farm and orchard are."

"That must have been incredible growing up."

Abby laughed. "Probably gave him plenty of space to get into lots of trouble."

I chuckled. "I can't imagine Nate ever getting into trouble."

Abby's eyes widened. "Oh, you need to ask around. Go have a chat with the Knox brothers, and they'll give you the inside scoop on Nate. They all went to school with him."

"Interesting."

"It's very entertaining and enlightening." She winked at me. "But, you probably don't care *that* much since you're not interested."

The door swung open, and a group of customers came

in, followed by Nate. He walked over and took a seat at my table and glanced at Abby before she went behind the counter.

"I've got good news about Millie. She's in stable condition. They're running a battery of tests, but nothing jarring yet."

Abby's brow quirked as she stared at Nate. "You came back to tell us that? You could have called." A smirk dashed across Abby's expression. "Is there any other reason you needed to stop by to deliver the news?"

She didn't wait for the answer as she wandered over to help the customers.

He shook his head. "I don't know what she's trying to imply."

"Beats me. I'm new around here."

Nate smiled and kept his eyes on mine a beat too long, creating a cyclone of emotion inside me. He blinked and glanced over at the counter. "That coffee cake looks good."

"It is." I grinned. "It's almost as good as those cupcakes."

His eyes stayed on mine. "If you say so."

I chuckled and looked around the coffee shop that felt more and more like home as the weeks went by. The rustic floors and exposed beams gave warmth to the café, and the new stone fireplace Abby installed in the corner made me never want to leave. Personally, Brielle could have her big mansions. I'd be perfectly happy in a one-room cabin like this one day, or maybe an old farmhouse with a porch that stretched along the sides of the old house.

I eyed Nate, wishing these feelings would just go away. "Abby told me your parents own a cherry orchard. That's incredible."

He nodded. "They do. It's mostly U-pick, and there are a few animals there. It's more like a haven for stray farm animals than anything."

"Is that where the mule wound up from yesterday?"

"Indeed." His smile widened. "Until we find its rightful owner."

"That's cool." I tapped my finger on the table, wanting to ask him so much more.

For some reason, I suddenly became interested in finding out everything about him. I couldn't picture him as anything other than the upstanding sheriff he appeared to be. Even when I closed my eyes and thought of a fourteen-year-old Nate, he was in his police uniform, reprimanding his teenage buddies.

I chuckled, and Nate scowled at me, which made him look even more sinfully delicious.

See?

I was doomed.

"What's so funny?"

"Nothing." I pursed my lips together to stop myself from telling him.

"Oh, come on. You've got to say now."

"Fine." I took a sip of my mocha and folded my arms over my chest. "I was just trying to picture you as a teenager."

"Why would you do that?"

I shrugged. "Had to do something to keep my mind off my worries."

His lips ticked up slightly on the left, and he kept his eyes on me. "And what did you come up with?"

I laughed. "That's the funny part. I can only picture you dressed like this..." I waved my hands around. "But plastered on a teenage boy getting everyone else in trouble."

He smoothed his fingers along his jawline and kicked his legs out in front of him. It was hard not to admire the strength in his body. Even his thighs looked strong and thick. I dragged my eyes away, and he caught me staring.

"Well, I can assure you that is the farthest from the truth you can get." He looked amused with my assessment.

"Oh, yeah? Enlighten me."

His lips moved to a near smile, but he stood from the table. "Duty calls, but maybe another time."

I shrugged. "Maybe. But thanks for telling me about Millie. It makes me feel marginally better."

"If it weren't for you seeing her, who knows how it could have played out?"

A few customers found tables around me. As I watched Nate slowly walk out of the coffee shop, I knew he'd become my new weakness.

I was just thrilled my sister was coming to keep me plenty occupied so I didn't do something stupid with my heart. She'd do a great job of talking some sense into me and pointing out all the reasons I shouldn't pay Nate a bit of attention. Abby already spelled it out clearly: Nate was married to his job and would forever be a bachelor.

A teenage girl I recognized as Izzy, Grace's daughter and Millie's great-granddaughter, bounded into the coffee shop with tear-stained cheeks.

"Kiddo, are you okay?" Abby asked, rushing over.

"Millie's in the hospital." She sniffled, and my heart ached.

"We know and are so sorry. And you, my dear, do not have to work today."

"But I need the school credit for my business class." She wiped her palm along her cheek.

Abby pulled her in. "You'll get it. You do more than

enough to earn your credit here. Now, go visit Millie at the hospital."

Izzy pulled back, and my heart melted at the sight of these ladies. There was just something so tight-knit about this town. Everyone watched over everyone else, and as I watched it unfold in front of me time and again, I caught myself craving it a little.

I always thought I loved getting to blend into the hustle and bustle of Chicago, but I wasn't so sure lately.

I stood and grabbed my drink. "I can drive you, Izzy. I'm not sure you should be behind the wheel with everything going on."

"Great idea, Amy." Abby nodded her head in agreement, rubbing Izzy's shoulders.

Izzy's eyes connected with mine, and I couldn't help but see how much she looked like her mom. "You wouldn't mind?" Her voice turned hoarse, and all I wanted was for Millie to be okay. These women needed her.

I smiled, nodding. "Not at all. It would give me something to do until my sister gets into town."

She sniffled with tears rimming her lids. "Thank you. I really appreciate it."

"Absolutely."

"And here..." Abby rushed behind the counter and

reached in for a mix of croissants, coffee cake, and muffins, putting them into a paper bag and setting them on the counter before she poured four cups of coffee, secured the lids, and put them in a carrier for us. "Take these to your mom and aunts."

I looped my purse over my shoulder and took the drink carrier as Izzy managed the rest.

On that note, we left for the hospital, but I wasn't prepared for what happened next.

Chapter Six

Nate

It was too obvious. Abby caught on right away. Why didn't I call to relay the news about Millie? Why did I feel this incessant need to show up and tell them? Because of Amy. I couldn't get her out of my head.

I couldn't afford to give any member of the Sunshine Breakfast Club ammo about Amy and me.

There was no Amy and me. There wouldn't be.

Abby loved to meddle in people's private lives, and I'd just handed her my heart on a silver platter. When Millie was back to feeling like herself again, there was no doubt that Tattletale Abby would be doing her best to inform her of my mistake.

I pulled up to the last property on my list and walked

up to the door. The crooked screen door creaked open before I even had a chance to knock, and Carol poked her head out.

"If it's about the roosters, Sheriff, I'm telling you I don't have any."

I hid a smile. We both knew that wasn't true, but today was not the day to deal with that violation.

"No, ma'am," I said with a slight nod. "That's not why I'm here today. I was hoping you might be able to ID something for me."

She let out a heavy sigh. "What did my husband do this time?"

I chuckled, knowing her husband had a bad habit of getting into a bit of trouble now and again.

"Everything's fine with Jerry," I assured her, opening the photos on my phone.

I held up the photo of the mule.

"What's this?" she asked, staring at my phone.

A chill blew some fresh snow onto the porch, and I kicked it off my boots.

"It's a mule that we're trying to return to its rightful owner. She's a bit of an escape artist. I was hoping you might know who owns her?"

Her thin lips got even thinner as they pushed into a tight smile, and she shook her head. "Nope. Don't have a clue.

Did you try Jeremy down the road?"

I nodded. "I did. Not his."

"Well, good luck there, Sheriff."

"Thanks, Carol. Have a good day."

"You too." She slammed the screen door, and I turned around and carefully made my way back to the SUV. It didn't look like Jerry had any plans to shovel or salt their walkway, and it was as slick as it could be.

I climbed into my vehicle and dialed my parents' number to let them know I'd been unsuccessful in finding the mule's owner.

As my mom answered the phone, I saw a red convertible—top down—screaming down the county road. It was twenty degrees outside. I couldn't even imagine how cold it was with the air blasting the driver. They had to be on something illegal to be that crazy, and I certainly couldn't allow that in Buttercup Lake.

"I gotta go. I'll call you back."

"Everything okay?"

"Yup."

I hung up, started the vehicle, and flipped the siren on as the car zoomed past me.

My jaw dropped open.

And I couldn't believe what I saw. In fact, I had to

squint my eyes to focus and believe who was behind the wheel.

Amy's strawberry blonde hair piled on top of her head, with a scarf tied around her chin, sped by as her mouth hung open. From all appearances, it looked like she was screaming or singing at the top of her lungs. Either way, something wasn't right.

I pulled out behind her and sped up.

She didn't pull over. Amy kept going.

Even with the siren blaring and the lights flashing.

Okay, I totally understood giving me a taste of my own medicine, but not like this.

She turned on her blinker and made a right onto the road leading to her home.

Unbelievable.

I shook my head, feeling my pulse rise. She was totally causing a scene.

As she slowed down, she didn't immediately pull into Brielle and Nick's home. Instead, it looked as if she were eyeing each house carefully until finally stopping in front of the one she belonged to.

Strange.

I had no idea what transpired between the coffee shop and here, but something didn't go well for her.

I flipped off my siren and pulled up behind her as she parked in the driveway.

Calling in the license plate to dispatch, I watched Amy bundle her black puffer coat as she glanced over her shoulder, scowling at me.

Letting out a deep breath, I climbed out of the SUV and walked over to Amy.

"Officer," she said dryly.

"It's Sheriff, but I'm pretty sure you're aware of that."

Her brows rose in feigned surprise. "Why would I know this?"

I stared at her, completely baffled. "Are we into role-playing now? I usually wait until further in the relationship before we do that."

She cocked her head slightly and narrowed her eyes on me but didn't take the bait. "Why did you pull me over?"

"Why did you *not* pull over?" I asked. "That's clearly going to get you in trouble."

"I don't know these roads very well, and I felt safer getting to where I was going." She pursed her lips together.

This didn't seem like the Amy I knew.

There was no attraction.

No allure.

No intrigue.

Maybe I really had talked myself out of falling for Amy.

"I don't have to answer any questions." She turned her head away and still gripped the steering wheel.

"I'm not arresting you."

She pointed her finger at me. "Yet."

"Well, with that attitude." I chuckled, shaking my head. "Why are you driving with the top down, and whose car is this? I don't recognize it. You didn't steal it, did you?"

Her mouth stayed closed as she shivered.

"Listen, you had me concerned. No one in their right mind would drive down a county road in arctic temperatures in a convertible with the top down. Least of whom... would be you. You are practical, cautious, and orderly."

"How do you know anything about me?" she quipped with an eye roll. "I wasn't speeding. I stopped at all stop signs. I didn't do anything wrong. So, you have no right to even be talking to me. You don't know me... at all."

I clicked my tongue as my brows furrowed in confusion, and then it spilled out. I knew it shouldn't have, but it did.

"I think we both know that I've seen more of you than most around here." I cleared my throat and looked over at the frozen lake in the distance. "Now, I'm just trying to make sure you weren't driving under the influence and endangering our community."

Her eyes turned livid. "Why would you ever think I'd do something like that? In the morning, of all times? I'm not answering any more of your questions."

"You haven't answered *any* of my questions," I pointed out.

She turned her nose at me.

"Then I have to ask you to take a field sobriety test," I said gently, knowing this was probably far more embarrassing for her than what happened in her bedroom.

"Under what pretense?" She turned her head to face me.

"Oh, I don't know. Driving with your top down, howling in the wind with twenty-degree temps. Call me delusional, but something like this doesn't exactly scream sober."

Amy's eyebrows rose as she climbed out of the convertible and stood in front of me. Folding her arms across her chest, she smirked.

"Tell me, Detective…"

"It's Sheriff," I corrected, unsure why Amy was getting such a rise out of ribbing me. This wasn't the woman I thought I knew.

She'd been right about that.

"Come on, Sheriff. Pull out your detective skills and come up with a possible scenario where I'm here, and you're there. You know *me*, but I clearly do not know *you*."

"I know you've been through a lot this morning, Amy." I shook my head. "So, I'm trying to give some leniency and allow for some grace to be given..." I stared at her. "But this isn't the Amy I know."

"You're right about that," she scoffed.

Okay. Clearly, the woman had two personalities, and I favored the other one.

But it was best to find this out now, not when I rolled over in bed to see the wrong one grinning at me, holding an axe or something.

Obviously, my job had made me more cautious than some, but it was like I was dealing with Dr. Jekyll and Mr. Hyde here.

"Alright, so I need you to take a step over—" As I started to give her instructions for the test, Amy's usual car rolled into the driveway.

My gaze snapped to the shadowy figure in the driver's seat when I saw a duplicate eye me from inside. She climbed out of her sedan and glanced at the look-a-like before turning her attention to me.

"What in the heck is going on here?" she asked.

I stared at the two identical women and couldn't believe what I was seeing.

Amy had a twin. Why hadn't she mentioned that?

Probably because we'd barely shared much in the way of conversation.

"Why is there a convertible parked in the driveway with the top down, and why does the town's sheriff look like he wants to arrest my sister?" Amy's gloved hands flew to her hips, but she couldn't really push through her puffy down jacket, so she just let them hang. "Seriously, Nate. What is going on?"

"You did not tell me you had a twin."

She shrugged. "It never came up."

"I am freezing. Can I get inside, please?" the other woman asked.

"You wouldn't be as cold had you not driven here with the top down."

Amy scrunched her nose. "Top down? Why in the world did you do that?"

Amy's sister stretched her arms toward the sky and smiled. "Because I hoped to catch pneumonia on my vacation."

Amy chuckled, and the kindness I'd been used to

surfaced as she glanced at me. "Will you cut her a break?"

"She still won't answer why she was driving with the top down."

"Is it illegal?" her twin asked.

"No."

"Oh, Alice. Quit messing with him. Just tell him why because I'm dying to know, too."

Alice walked to the trunk of the convertible, opened it up, and grabbed her bag before fishing in the outside pocket for a knit cap. She pulled the red hat over her ears and let out a huff.

"I flew into the Podunk airport a town over that was supposed to have plenty of rental cars." She twisted her lips into a snarl. "And when I got there, the guy was already wrapping up to leave and said they only had this convertible available, so I took it."

"Oh, my gosh. You could have called me," Amy said, giggling.

"Then, as I made my way onto the wrong county road, I somehow managed to get the top down, so I pulled over and couldn't get it back up."

I tried with everything I had not to start laughing. I looked at the sky, the lake... Amy.

"And so, I decided if I could just make it ten more

miles to your place, I'd be fine. Next thing I know, Detective Clouseau here got behind me and put on his flashers."

"Sirens," I corrected. "And most people pull over when they go on."

Amy chuckled.

Alice stared at me. "I'm not most people."

"Clearly."

"Anyway, that's why I'm here and about to go into the final state of hypothermia."

I scratched my chin and let out a sigh. "You know, had you told me even half that story when I came over to this little red number, I would have hopped back in my patrol car and left you alone."

Her sister tipped her chin slightly and grinned. "But don't you think this was far more fun, Officer?"

"He's the sheriff," Amy corrected, giving me a quick glance.

"Thanks, Amy." I drew a deep breath and glanced at my SUV. "I'll be on my way."

Alice had already rolled her luggage to the front door.

"Sorry about all this. Alice isn't usually this testy. She hates small planes, small towns, and her first serious relationship was with a police officer."

I chuckled. "Wonderful. She'll love Buttercup Lake."

"Anyway, you might already know this, but I have an update on Millie."

"Oh, yeah?" I hadn't had time to check on her since my search for the mule's owner and Alice's shenanigans. "How's she doing?"

"Well, she didn't slip," Amy said softly. "She had a mild stroke. That's why she went down so quickly and didn't seem to really know what happened."

"Oh, no." A heaviness sat on my chest at the thought of Millie and her granddaughters. "How's everyone holding up?"

"Well, actually, quite well. Millie seemed to take this as a sign."

"A sign?" I shook my head. "How so?"

"Apparently, her own mother had a stroke when she was ninety and still lived to over a hundred. She figures if this one didn't take her, she's meant to be here a lot longer."

"That's Millie, alright. Did they say how long she'll be in the hospital?"

"Sounds like it just depends on what the tests reveal."

"Wow. Well, I'm glad she's got such a positive attitude."

"It's the only way to fly," Amy said cheerfully.

"Come on, Amy. Enough flirting with Clouseau."

I grimaced. "Have fun visiting your sister."

She chuckled as I turned to make my way to my patrol vehicle and wondered how there could possibly be two Amys when I couldn't even handle one.

Chapter Seven

Amy

"Please tell me that's not the policeman you have a crush on."

I stared at my sister, who had a light blue tint to her lips. "Define crush."

She fell back onto the couch in the large great room overlooking the lake. "Oh, Amy. He's got *Unavailable* stamped all over his forehead."

I pulled a pink chenille blanket out of a chest and gave it to her. "How do you figure?"

"He didn't flirt with me at all. Not. At. All."

I laughed and sat next to her, lifting the cup of tea I'd made. "Has that never happened in your world before? You are used to stepping out the door, and men falling at your feet?"

"If he thought I was you, why wasn't he flirting with me?"

"Well, because you looked like you'd smoked some wacky tobacky for you to be in a convertible with the top down, cruising along a county road in the dead of winter. Not to mention he'd just seen me earlier, and I appeared okay. He was probably genuinely concerned."

She leaned forward for her own tea and sniffed the peppermint aroma lifting from the steaming cup. "Did you sleep together?"

I smacked the expensive throw pillow next to me. "What? Why would you think that?"

"You saw him already today..." She shrugged. "I remember how it worked in small towns like this. People get bored. Maybe you woke up with him. He's already seen you naked. Besides, once he saw you, his eyes lit up like someone who, you know, either has a really good imagination or..."

I stared at my sister. At times like this, it was hard to remember that we were identical twins.

"He's a professional."

"Who either imagines you in the nude or has seen you that way."

"Says who?" I rolled my eyes.

"We look alike. I know these things. And you didn't answer my question."

"So you think we all just have sex with one another to keep ourselves amused up here?" I shook my head. "You're more scarred about small-town living than I am."

"I'm not scarred. I'm realistic. Tell me." She eyed me. "What do you do on a Friday night?"

I chuckled. "That's easy. I do the same thing I did in Chicago. I grab a book, make some popcorn, pour some wine, and… read."

"You're not a good example." She shook her head and took a sip. "What do you think the sheriff does on a Friday night?"

"I don't know. There's a new bowling alley in town. Maybe he goes there."

"Bowling?" Her eyes stayed on mine in disbelief.

"What? It's a really nice one."

"You've been?"

I nodded. "Don't be a snob. Buttercup Lake is… different. It's nothing like how we grew up. People here care about one another. They take care of each other."

"If you say so."

"I *know* so."

"Are you going soft on me?" she asked, smiling.

"No, but I'm just saying it's not all terrible being somewhere that is kind."

We had a crappy childhood. There was no sugarcoating the way we grew up.

The idea of nurturing never crossed our parents' minds, and that was the kind explanation.

They weren't the worst, but they certainly didn't try their best. Of course, my sister thinks I give them way too much leniency, but I moved away so I could.

The idea of living with the heaviness of not feeling loved by the two people in the world who should love you most wasn't anything I truly wanted to bear. So, I packaged up all the anger, hurt, and animosity and buried it deep.

So deep, in fact, that when I visited my mom and dad and smelled the stale cigarette smoke in the walls of their trailer, I no longer became angry.

Just sad.

I wanted to believe they put Alice and me first, or at the very least, second, but I knew from experience that we'd always been pretty far down the list. If they needed cigarettes and we needed lunch money, they were the ones out back smoking on the stoop.

It turned out we represented disappointment to them from the moment we were born. Somehow, they went through the nine months of Mom being pregnant thinking we were boys. And by boys, I mean high school quarterbacks who'd carry on my dad's tradition of playing in the same small town he was born and raised in.

The same one we couldn't wait to escape.

All because my mom didn't like being reprimanded for smoking during the pregnancy. Her solution had been simple—just don't go back to the doctor.

It was one of the things that had drawn me to Leo. We'd both come from families who'd rather we just grew up and left, and it made it easy to become fast friends. We'd been inseparable until we weren't. The ache in my chest sharpened as I pushed the images away from this morning and Millie. It was incredible how moments and things that seemed so unalike could trigger memories to permeate every cell and create a prison of inescapable thoughts.

But that part of my life, thankfully, was over. I just always prayed that telling my mom about my new job wouldn't somehow find its way back to him. Not that he'd care. But I knew he still felt trapped. I would if I were him. The poverty of that small town rained down on the most vulnerable, and Leo had become most definitely susceptible to everything that scared me about a small town.

And it wasn't that our family was necessarily poor, but we went without so our parents could go with. By that, I mean my mom would buy some designer purse to sling over her shoulder for a Saturday night out, or my dad would buy some flashy motorcycle he'd never ride. Meanwhile, our coats were too small and our shoes squished our toes.

To top it off, it was obvious. All the kids knew that our parents didn't really care, and for some reason, in turn, neither did they.

I'd never forget my dad telling me he was finally going to show up to one of my volleyball games. I'd told the entire team. None of them believed me because they knew my parents usually hung out at the local dive bar the moment my dad got off work, right during the heart of game time. But for some reason, I actually believed him.

Until the last buzzer sounded, and my sister grabbed all my stuff out of the locker room and met me outside before I burst into tears.

And Leo was there to pick up the pieces too.

My sister sighed and broke me from my spiraling thoughts.

"I'm sure I won't be here much longer," I told her, shaking the suffocating feelings floating over me. Maybe she was right. I was only seeing the good of this place, but the bad was lurking right around the corner.

She propped herself up on her elbow and sipped the tea. Her gaze skimmed the top of the cup as she looked at me. "What do you mean? I thought you thought this was a long-term position."

I shrugged. "I could be wrong, but I just found out that Brielle and Nick will be out of the country for a long time and Hunter and Daisy will be watching Tate, and they barely need me."

"Right. But when Brielle is in town, it's an entirely different story."

"True." I looked out the window to see a couple of new ice fishing holes. The dark spots were easy to spot in the sea of sparkling white. "I bet this place is gorgeous in the summer."

"You'll find out," she reminded me.

I stretched my legs out in front of me and sighed. I hoped that was the case.

My sister spotted the book I'd been reading for the book club on the coffee table. "Is it good?"

"Yeah. It's awesome." I nodded. "It's for the book club I belong to."

My sister flashed me a knowing grin. "You're certainly making yourself right at home here, aren't you?

What was all that hemming and hawing before you moved here? You didn't want to leave the city and all that."

"I guess it's what is called… growth." I eyed my sister.

My sister shuddered and laughed. "I wouldn't know."

I tossed a pillow at her, and she dodged it. "You're so full of it. I'll make you a deal."

"Lemme have it." She motioned with her hands.

"I bet by the end of the week that you'll want to come back."

She scrunched her nose. "Only to see you."

I shook my head. "Nope. I mean to vacation here."

She yawned and stared out the window as snowflakes swirled through the air. "You've got your work cut out for you then because so far, my welcome here hasn't been the greatest."

"Go easy on the sheriff," I teased.

"Listen, I know he's absolutely gorgeous and could be the model for some lumberjack magazine out there, but that doesn't make the outcome any better."

My brow lifted. "All because he didn't flirt with you?"

"He was willing to arrest me even though he thought I was you. If that doesn't scream emotionally unavailable and not boyfriend material, I don't know what would."

"First of all, I'm happy he's not a crooked cop. I don't need leniency." I laughed. "And second of all, I don't think he was planning on arresting you. I got the feeling he just wanted to see what was going on. Besides, I had a rough morning, and he probably thought I had a mental breakdown."

"Why would he think that?"

"Because one of my friends, a sweet older lady, went down like a ton of bricks this morning. I was the one there when it happened and called emergency services."

Alice's hand shot to her mouth. "Are you serious?"

I nodded. "Yup. I was shaking, and we'd just spent the night before together at the book club."

She reached over and clutched my hands. "I'm so sorry. If I knew you'd gone through that, I would have lightened up a bit too." She let out a reflective sigh.

"It just dredged up old memories of things I'd thought I'd forgotten about."

My sister gave me a sympathetic smile and shook her head. "You can't just forget things like that. Leo changed... everything."

I nodded, knowing exactly what she meant.

"I know you get attached easily," she said, glancing at me.

I let the comment slide. "It's not that."

She changed topics. "Well, I can see why you think it's absolutely beautiful here. Even though everything is covered in snow and the bumpy landing at the airport left something to be desired, there is something oddly peaceful about being here." She looked around my temporary home. "And this house is what dreams are made of."

I chuckled. "Yeah, it's a pretty amazing perk. A little too big for me, but still pretty cool."

Alice tipped her chin up and let out a deep breath. "Can you believe how things have worked out in our lives?"

"You mean that we're both decent human beings even though we had a lack of guidance?"

She chuckled. "Lack of guidance? You always have a knack for making things seem better than they were."

I shrugged. "Why hold onto everything? But no, I am amazed we made it out okay."

She straightened on the couch and grinned. "You want to know why we did?"

"Why?"

"Because we are badass women." She nodded. "We don't compromise."

"Is that more of a you thing or...?" My brows lifted.

"Oh, come on. Amy, you're the baddest one I know.

Think about all the men you've left because you won't put up with their crap."

I chuckled and shook my head. "I don't exactly see it that way. There comes a point when I have to be real with myself. When I must understand that I'm the problem. Time and again, I pick the bad seeds."

"Nonsense." She shook her head. "It takes strength not to stay in a bad situation."

"I completely agree about that, but I keep finding the bad situations, and then I dive right in, headfirst." My shoulders tensed as my mind skated over to Nate. "But I'm determined to change that."

"Of course you are."

"So, how's your boyfriend doing?" I asked, happy to change the subject.

"Amazing. He's about to turn in his thesis. Once he hits *Submit*, he said he might come on up here."

"No way."

"Yup, and he's got a job all lined up in Chicago. I think..." She drew in a breath and squinted her eyes shut. "I think he might even pop the question."

I squealed with happiness the moment the words left her lips. "You think?"

"I may or may not have seen a receipt tucked in a

drawer to a jewelry store that begins with a T."

"No. Way." I sprang up from the couch and wrapped my arms around her neck.

"I have to admit there were times I was worried we'd get to the end of all his schooling and then he'd book. No pun intended."

I grimaced. "George would never do that to you."

"I'm a lot to handle."

"Nah. Not for the right guy, and George is that one."

She nodded and smiled slowly. "What are the plans this afternoon?"

"Well, I wanted to take you down to the main street in town, but with Millie in the hospital, I'm not sure that's a great idea."

My sister looked puzzled. "Why? Does she own all the stores or something?"

I laughed and shook my head. "No, but I just…" I shrugged. "I can't help but think there's something I could be doing to help her and her family. Plus, the really awesome antique store is owned by her granddaughter, and I want you to meet her." I twisted my lips into a contemplative frown. "In fact, I think I'm going to call Daisy and see if there's anything we can do."

My sister nodded and stood from the couch. "Sure.

Sounds like a plan. Did you want any more tea? I'm going to make some."

"I'd love some."

Alice wandered off toward the kitchen, and I reached for my cellphone, dialing Daisy.

She picked up immediately, and I started telling her my ideas immediately.

Chapter Eight

Nate

"Your mother named her Lucky," my dad informed me.

I pulled off my gloves and kicked off my boots in the entryway as my dad did the same.

"Fitting name."

"So, you think we're off the hook for finding the owner?" he asked.

I nodded. "It's been a week. I have a feeling whoever had her let her go on purpose."

"And in the brutal winter," my dad muttered. "I just don't understand people sometimes."

"Me neither, Dad."

He looked up at me. "It's why I never wanted to be a

cop, you know."

No. I didn't know.

I actually never understood why my dad didn't want to follow in grandpa's footsteps. I just knew he wanted to farm.

"I always wondered."

We wandered into my family room, and my dad took a seat with a grunt.

"You okay?" I asked.

"Just the back still."

"You might want to get it looked at," I offered.

"So they can tell me to take some Ibuprofen and stay in bed for the winter? I think not. I need that money to feed the mule now," he teased with a wink.

"Want some coffee?"

"Do you have any of that espresso stuff?"

I chuckled. "I do. I'll make us both one."

My dad looked extremely happy—tired, but extremely happy. He slowly stretched his legs and gingerly brought them back in, careful not to tweak his back.

"So, how'd you say you did that again?" The last time I'd asked, he was a little shifty.

I packed the grounds and pulled a double shot as I glanced over at my dad.

"I don't remember. Getting the laundry out of the dryer or something."

My brow arched. "That's not what I remembered you saying."

"I don't know what you're getting at." He frowned in my direction.

"You know, just wondering how you really hurt your back." I brought over a cup of his espresso and handed it to him.

"You can't handle the truth of it, Son." He chuckled. "You just can't."

"I've seen a lot in my life, Dad. I think I'll be fine."

"You won't. Trust me." He took a sip of the espresso as I wandered back into the kitchen to make mine.

I waited until the espresso machine had stopped and sat across from my dad, lifting my feet onto a leather ottoman.

"So, you said you didn't want to be a cop because people disappointed you?"

"Indeed." He gave a quick nod. "Some of the people I knew best disappointed me the most."

"And it scarred you for life."

"Absolutely did." He finished his espresso. "It all started back in fifth grade. My best friend stole my GI Joe figurine."

I would have laughed, but my dad looked deadly serious.

"I cut him some slack when he returned him with a handwritten note, forced by his parents, accompanied it. By junior high school, two other friends stole a dirt bike and busted it up over at Devil's Cliff. Once high school hit and my best friend stole my girlfriend, I'd had it with the human race." He smiled and glanced out the window. "But had all that not happened, I wouldn't have met your mom."

"I thought you met Mom at a football game."

He nodded. "I did. I'd snuck into the locker room before the game and sprinkled itching powder into the guy's jockstrap who stole my girlfriend. Your mom happened to bump into me on my way out. She asked why I looked so guilty. I told her, and she grabbed the container, marched inside, and sprinkled some more inside the guy's..." He started laughing, wiping his eyes. "Well, you get the picture. I knew we were meant to be."

"You and Mom did that?" My eyes widened. "Where did you even get that stuff?"

"Oh, your grandpa told me about a guy who got in trouble once when he was in high school for sprinkling the stuff on a teacher's chair."

My brows rose. "And you wanted to be that guy."

"Well, it didn't exactly feel great to have your best friend steal your gal, even if it did work out better in the end. Your mom is a real catch. I just… I needed that vengeance, and because I did, I was pretty certain farm life might be better than putting on a uniform for me."

I chuckled, nodding. "I can't believe you never told me about the itching powder."

He grinned. "I didn't want to get arrested by Grandpa or you."

"Very funny. There's nothing illegal about it unless he died."

"I'm sure he wanted to with all his dancing and squirming on the field like that in front of the whole high school."

"But I wouldn't trade it for the world. I never would have married your mom or had you and your brother."

I nodded in agreement, glancing outside to see snow skating through the air from the breeze picking up.

He cleared his throat. "Speaking of, have you ever thought of settling down sometime? I know you never felt you had time or… I don't know what it was truly holding you back, but…" He didn't say anything else.

"I just don't think I'm the settling-down type. I have a lot going on around town, and I don't see how I could give a hundred percent to a relationship. It wouldn't be fair to the woman." It made perfect sense to me.

"Ah, I see. How admirable." A smirk surfaced on my dad's face. "Is that the only reason?"

"Yeah."

"Your brother told me the same thing, and then he found his partner in life, so I'm not giving up just yet."

"Don't hold your breath, Dad." I shook my head. "My brother and I aren't that alike."

He scratched his chin and grunted as he moved. "I know. I also know how fulfilling my life has been with your mother and both of my sons over the years. I don't want you hitting my age and realizing you missed out."

The same thought had occurred to me more than once. "I'd be lying if I didn't say that it wouldn't be nice to come home to a house that wasn't empty, to share a morning cup of coffee with someone other than myself, wind down in the family room after work with someone who understood my day."

"Doesn't sound like you've given it much thought," my dad teased.

"But I'm also well aware that there are many nights when I get called out of bed and holidays I'm needed someplace other than home."

"Listen, unlike your mom, I'm not going to keep pestering you about this. But, just so you know…" He smiled at me. "When you find the right person, they don't mind that you must leave because of your job. In fact, they're proud of you for it."

"I'll keep that in mind."

"What are we doing for dinner tonight?" my dad asked, glancing at me with a wry smile.

"We?"

"She's off at her knitting group, and I don't feel like cooking with this back issue of mine."

"Good to know." I stood from the chair and chuckled as I walked to the kitchen and opened the freezer. "I'd planned on making some baked cod. I'll just pull two filets from the freezer."

"Thanks, Son."

As I made my way to the cabinet to pull out a bowl to quicky defrost the fish, the doorbell rang.

"You expecting someone?" my dad called over his shoulder. "Did I interfere with your bachelorhood?"

"Dad, I don't know where you think we live, but we have better odds of Lucky coming up to my porch and ringing the doorbell rather than my future bride."

My dad shook his head as I walked over to the front

door and answered, surprised to see Amy bundled up on the other side of the threshold.

"I have a dilemma." She grimaced and glanced around the porch with a shiver.

"Did your car break down? Is your sister sunning on the beach in the snowstorm and wants to argue with you? What are we talking?" I narrowed my eyes on her. "You are Amy, right?"

The truth was that I knew it was Amy without a shadow of a doubt. The moment her eyes connected with mine, I felt an instant charge.

She smiled, tipping her chin slightly as she glanced over my shoulder. "Am I interrupting anything?"

"Would it matter?" I teased.

"Are you going to make the poor woman freeze to death? Let her in," my dad barked from behind.

"Come on in," I said, ushering her inside. "Or you'll let all the heat out."

As she stepped by me, the familiar vanilla scent lingered. "So, what's up?"

"I wouldn't usually just knock on the sheriff's door at dinnertime, but I hit a bit of a snag."

"If one of my men pulled your sister over, there's nothing I can do about it."

Her lips curved into a smile. "She's not that bad."

"She's nothing like you."

Her brows rose. "Thank you. I think?"

I gave a quick nod.

"Anyway, I'd stopped by the police station to fill out the paperwork for a parade and gathering this Saturday, but Flo told me it couldn't be done because the station needed at least five business days, and the only way to get a permit issued was to speak directly with the sheriff, which is you."

"Did she," I said flatly.

I knew full well that Flo made a habit of issuing parade permits within hours of the intended time just to watch my men hop into line.

"What's it for?" I asked, genuinely curious.

"Well, it's been confirmed that Millie is coming home on Saturday, and the Sunshine Breakfast Club wanted her to know how important she is to the town. We thought we could do a quick parade and a nice bazaar at the community center to help raise funds for her care."

The kindness sweeping through Amy's eyes told me everything. This had been her idea.

"It's supposed to be in the thirties, so at least it won't be too cold," she added, shuffling papers in her bag. She pulled out the small form I recognized and pushed it into my hands. "My hope is that you'll bend this little rule and let us host the events for Millie."

I could see the hope pulsing through her, and it was hard to look away. Her soft brown eyes silently pleaded with me as silence filled the room.

"Did you want a police escort or anything to accompany the parade?" I grabbed the pen out of my pocket and placed the form on the wall, scribbling my name on the bottom.

"You'd do that?"

"Sure. What were you planning?"

"Bob, down the road, has a couple of tractors his boys were going to decorate and drive. The classic car club had about eight members volunteer to drive their classics, and of course, we have the football team and cheerleaders coming out with the marching band. Izzy is working with the art department at the high school to do the banners, and her business club is putting together the donation sites for food and money." She let out a deep breath. "Millie is doing incredibly well, but there are some modifications that they want to make on the house to make things easier."

I nodded, debating whether I should mention one little issue.

"Anyway, I can't thank you enough for bending the

rules to make this happen." Her eyes stayed on mine, and I felt the familiar pull to her.

"Anything for Millie. How are her granddaughters holding up? And Jackson Sr.?"

"Pretty good. They've made sure there's someone with Millie nonstop at the hospital."

"That fact alone probably riles up Millie."

"Jackson looks exhausted, but he's been amazing." She rocked back on the heels of her boots and looked around, smiling. "I'll let you get back to dinner, and I'm sorry about barging in. This is just really important."

"Absolutely," I said, nodding.

Amy turned around and opened the door as I reached to hold it open for her. A cold gust of air blasted into the house as she glanced over her shoulder. "Thanks again."

I closed the door and leaned against it for a few seconds, closing my eyes and taking a deep breath.

It was one thing to ignore Amy's beauty, but to experience how kind her heart was didn't make things easy.

"Why didn't you invite her to dinner, for crying out loud?" my dad asked, walking over to the foyer as I turned around.

"Her sister's in town," I muttered, making my way to the kitchen. "And I don't know her that well."

"That's the point in inviting her for dinner. To get to know her."

"Dad, it's not like that." I shook my head and let out a silent sigh as I tried to wrap my head around the feelings washing over me.

But I knew the best course of action was inaction, and I was determined to make sure I was actively as inactive as possible around Amy, or I'd probably do something really dumb... like invite her to dinner.

Chapter Nine

Amy

I didn't understand it. My sister's boyfriend flew in last night. It was like they couldn't bear to be apart... for even a few days?

Whatever.

I was happy for her that they were in love, yada-yada.

And I was looking forward to a dinner out with them tonight.

Her boyfriend was a good guy, but still. I seriously couldn't understand wanting to be around a guy that much, even if I were dating him.

My mind coincidentally flipped back to Nate.

He might be different. The problem was that I'd always found guys who couldn't stop moving. They just had to go, go, go. In hindsight, I think they were running away from something or were on something. Who knew nowadays? But it would be nice to find someone who had the same pace I did.

He'd seemed so relaxed when I'd stopped by his house last night, but it also felt like he couldn't wait to sign whatever I had for him so I'd leave.

That was kind of getting to be a pattern.

But I didn't want to overthink things. It was sweet of him to offer up some officers for the parade. Sirens and lights always livened up an event.

Millie was improving by leaps and bounds, and I was thrilled that she'd be able to see what the town was doing for her.

I glanced at Daisy, who was talking to Izzy about the signage the high school class was constructing and wondered if it always felt this good to live here. For the first time in my life, I felt like I belonged. It was a foreign sensation, but I wasn't completely sure I could get used to it.

Daisy held up a colorful sign that read *Welcome Home* and grinned.

"Love it," I said, glancing at Millie's great-granddaughter. "How are you holding up?"

Izzy grinned and nodded. "I'm still trying to wrap my

head around her having a stroke. I know they said it was mild, but I just never expected it. Millie assured us over and over again that she is fine, and this was just a sign to live each day to the fullest."

"She's an incredible woman," I said, smiling.

Izzy nodded. "And we're all pretty sure Millie is going to get all fired up about this parade."

"In a good way?" I glanced at Daisy before returning my gaze back to Izzy.

"To be determined." Izzy chuckled. "But she got wind of it because people in this town just can't keep their mouths shut, and she said she wants all donations to go to the food bank because she has plenty of food in the pantry and coins in the bank, but she wouldn't turn down an occasional casserole or two for her and Jackson. I don't think she has any idea about the parade or bazaar, though."

"Thank goodness Saturday is only a couple of days away." Daisy smiled. "Speaking of, Tate's coming home early. They're cutting their Arizona trip short so they can get a move on it to Japan."

"That's so exciting." And it will give me the perfect reason to quit thinking about Nate. "When's the little fellow get here?"

"Sunday."

"That's great. My sister can meet him."

"I heard Nate pulled over your sister thinking it was you," Daisy said, dipping her brush into a tub of red paint. "That must have been something."

"Yes, and she didn't make it easy on him. She pulled the oldest twin trick in the book and didn't give him a hint that she was my twin sister." I walked over to the sink to wash my hands. "Unfortunately, my sister hates small towns. We grew up in one that wasn't exactly all rainbows and butterflies. She's very skeptical."

"I like her already," Daisy joked. "Do you mind if I throw together a little gathering in her honor Friday, maybe just drinks and appetizers or a light dinner?"

"Really? You'd do that?"

She looked surprised. "Of course, and we can go over final details for Millie's homecoming on Saturday."

"My sister is going to be shocked."

"Should I make a sign for her too?" Izzy teased.

I wiped off my hands and wandered over to Daisy. "What time on Sunday is Tate arriving with Brielle?"

"It sounds like they plan on getting in early morning, but you don't have to worry about a thing. Hunter already has big plans." She chuckled. "He bought a cute little fishing pole that is still too big for Tate and is meeting his buddy at some fancy ice hut with heat and food. I doubt the line will ever make it under the ice, but I think it's Hunter's way of showing him off with the boys."

"Aww." I chuckled, touching my chest. "Hunter is such a good daddy."

"He really is. It makes me excited for one day."

"And it gives the rest of us hope," I teased.

"So, you aren't completely against dating?" she asked.

"No, I mean, not really. I just don't trust myself at this point."

Daisy cocked her head slightly. "What do you mean, you don't trust yourself?"

"I'm not sure I really know how to pick a solid guy. I tend to go for the bad boys or..." I shrugged, glancing at Izzy. "Cover your ears, Izzy."

Izzy pretended to put her palms on each side of her head.

"Or I zero in on the physical stuff." I playfully scowled. "Okay, I'm done, Izzy."

She flashed a funny grin. "That was all you had to say? I've read worse in my romance books."

I laughed and shook my head. "Anyway, I'd love to find my Mr. Right someday, but I've learned to become extremely happy with myself in the meantime. I'm very good company."

Izzy chuckled. "That's what I found. It wasn't until I was comfortable in my own skin that Caleb came my way, and I'm so happy he did."

Ah, teenage love.

"You two are really cute together."

Daisy nodded in agreement.

"Is there anything else I can help with?" I asked.

Daisy and Izzy shook their heads.

"I'm dropping Izzy off with her mom in a little bit, and then I'm home to get everything ready for Tate."

"Please text me how I can help later. I'm so excited to see him again."

"Will do." Daisy waved, and I turned around to make my way to dinner with my sister and boyfriend.

We were meeting at the Buttercup Lodge's restaurant, where Daisy actually used to bartend. The more casual area had great burgers, and the fine dining was out of this world. Brielle and Nick loved going there, and that was another fun perk of being Tate's nanny.

The moment I stepped into the cozy, dimly lit restaurant, a flurry of anticipation stirred. I spotted my sister and her boyfriend, George, seated at a comfy corner booth, and my sister excitedly waved.

When I got there, George stood and gave me a hug and a quick kiss on each cheek.

"This place makes the best Moscow Mules," he informed me. "Way better than anything you can get back in Chicago." He smiled and took a seat as I slid in next to my sister.

He leaned over and smooched her, and I couldn't help but love their affectionate display. It was really nice to see familiar faces tonight.

"See? This place might sneak up on you before you know it," I teased.

The restaurant hummed with murmurs, an occasional glass clinking, and the soft play of music. Our server came over, and I ordered tea and sparkling water.

My sister leaned over and squeezed me. "While you were painting signs, George drove me to the cutest petting zoo ever."

"Oh, yeah? Where's that?"

"Just on the other side of the lake. It's connected to a lodge or something called Honey Leaf or I don't know. Anyway, it's a really cute place. You should take Tate when it warms up."

George ordered several appetizers while I glanced at

the menu. I wasn't sure why I bothered since I ordered the same thing every time I came. It was so nice to be with my sister. Buttercup Lake had really started to feel like home, but there was no doubt that I missed hanging out with my sister.

Right when I'd settled on the bacon cheeseburger, the energy in the room shifted, and I glanced over at the hostess, who lit up like a fireworks show. My eyes fell to the man she was staring at.

"What's got you grinning from ear to ear?" my sister asked.

My smile dropped the moment I realized my subconscious reaction to the sheriff.

I turned my gaze back to her. "I was smiling?"

"And now I know why."

"Oh, is that the hunk Amy's got the hots for?" George joked.

"Do you tell him everything?" I teased, and my sister nodded.

I cocked my head slightly and winked at George. "I'd be careful there if I were you. You're not family yet."

George laughed and nodded. "Yeah. She's getting extremely testy. Must be the right sheriff."

"I don't have the hots for anyone," I whispered as he walked into the dining area.

My heart skipped a beat and then ten more as he walked by our table. Time slid into a murky wasteland of confusion. I started fiddling with my napkin and realized I was probably looking at Nate like he had three heads.

But before he sat down, he turned suddenly and stepped back to our table.

"Hey, it's the twins." His smile made me feel all gushy inside, and I wanted to just slide under the table because, undoubtedly, my facial expressions were as transparent as everything else in my life.

My palms grew clammy, and I ripped my gaze from his and stared at my sister, hoping she'd say something for the both of us while I caught my breath.

She didn't.

"Fancy seeing you here," I said breathily, which made George chuckle.

"It's one of my favorites," he said, glancing at my sister and her boyfriend. He stuck out his hand to George. "I'm Nate. Your girlfriend probably filled you in on our encounter."

George nodded and smiled. "Maybe a little. But I do thank you for putting the convertible top back up for her."

I glanced at my sister. "He did?"

She nodded. "Apparently, when we went inside, he

must have done it."

I glanced at Nate. "Thanks."

"All in a day's work."

"Not just because you're nice?" I asked.

"I'm not that nice. Duty calls more than anything," he joked.

My sister kicked me under the table, but I didn't know what she wanted me to do.

So, I did what any loving sister would do and kicked her back.

She flinched as George stared between us. "You two okay?"

"I heard you're putting a lot of time into making things perfect for when Millie comes home on Saturday. That's really sweet of you."

"Ah, it's nothing. Thanks for lending some policemen for the parade."

"It's the least I can do. Millie's done a lot for this town." His smile was undeniably the sexiest smile I'd ever seen. I could look at it for hours.

"I'd better get over to the table before my date shows up," he said slowly.

His words snatched me right out of the happiness bubble I'd been in.

A date?

I thought he was married to his work.

"Yeah. We wouldn't want you to make a bad impression," I said grumpily.

Nate's hazel eyes stayed on mine, and my cheeks flushed. If I didn't know better, it felt like everything and everyone else in the room had just drifted away, leaving us.

But regardless of the twinkle in his eyes, he smiled and made his way to his table and sat down.

To wait for a date.

"I think things have become crystal clear about why you're still single." My sister shook her head as the appetizers came to the table.

I rolled my eyes. "I'm not that bad."

"Not usually, but this was something else."

My brows furrowed. "What's that supposed to mean?"

"I think you're falling for him."

"Not even a little." I shook my head and dug into a cheese curd.

I glanced at him as a woman came to the table, and I couldn't help but smile.

Chapter Ten

Nate

Damn.

Beautiful and kind.

I chuckled, watching Amy walk into Daisy and Hunter's living room with her sister and her boyfriend. I took a sip of beer and dragged my gaze away. It didn't help that my mom noticed me glancing at Amy a few times when we'd met for dinner at the lodge.

Amy's eyes caught mine, and I raised my beer in her direction, suddenly feeling like I was at a frat party. She smiled, and a little dimple surfaced on her right cheek as she pulled off her knit cap and matching red scarf.

The fire roaring next to me in Hunter and Daisy's stone fireplace made me sweat as I watched Amy chatting with Daisy. I stepped a couple of feet away and quickly realized it wasn't the fire.

"Sheriff." Millie's voice surprised me, and I spun around to see her sitting in a chair.

"Millie, I didn't see you there."

"Well, you should have, considering what you do for a living." She eyed me playfully. "I see what's going on there."

"On where?" I took a sip of beer.

"The twins."

"Aren't you supposed to be in the hospital?" I teased.

"I couldn't stand it one more second, and I think they knew I meant business when the nurses asked me to do two laps around the nurses' station, and I did ten."

"Wow, Millie." I nodded, impressed. "I'd ask how you're feeling, but it sounds like you're doing really well."

"Sure. Considering all things. I'd say it was a wake-up call, but I'm old." She shrugged. "And it's expected."

"I can assure you, none of us expected it. You're in better health than ninety percent of the town."

She giggled and shook her head. "Well, I can't go yet. My work isn't done." Her eyes fell on Amy, and I laughed.

"So, you are responsible for the mule."

"Can't blame me for seeing Amy in the nude. I didn't

expect you to go peeping around there when I sent in the mule."

The room fell silent, and Amy's cheeks flushed.

Millie glanced around the room. "Oh, don't give me that. You all heard about the mule incident."

Daisy chuckled, nodding, while Grace walked over to Millie with a smile.

It had to have been Flo.

"For the record, I did not see Amy in the buff." I looked around the room and realized that absolutely nobody believed me.

"Would anyone like some little smokies?" Daisy asked, holding a tray of tiny sausages with toothpicks coming out of each one.

"I'll take some," Millie said.

Grace touched her grandma's shoulder. "Are you sure you should be having sausage right now?"

"I didn't get to my age without some fatty substances now and again. I need strength."

Daisy eyed Grace and wandered over with the tray as Millie reached for a toothpick.

I scooted away and over to Amy, who looked oddly at peace.

"I'm so sorry about that. It had to have been Flo, the

receptionist," I whispered. "I haven't told a soul."

Amy shook her head and chuckled. "I knew it was only a matter of time."

Hunter walked into the family room with a bowl of chips. "What did I miss?"

"You know, the mule story…" Millie's brows rose up and down.

Daisy cleared her throat. "Okay, everyone. We have a buffet set up in the kitchen with some light appetizers, but I wanted to take this moment to welcome Amy's sister, Alice, and Alice's boyfriend, George. Amy has been such an amazing addition to our town, and it's so nice to see there are two of her."

Alice laughed and wrapped her arm around Amy. "She's the nice one, though."

"Not true," Amy said, shaking her head. "But thanks, Daisy. I wasn't sure about small-town living, but I've really fallen in love with the people and this place. I've just learned to shut my blinds if the sheriff is in my part of town."

I chuckled as Amy glanced at me, and it felt like the world stopped. I choked down the rest of my beer before she started again.

"And tonight shouldn't be about my sister or me. We need to start celebrating early that Millie is home from the hospital." Amy clapped and turned to see Millie sitting in her chair with a sausage in her mouth, and the room erupted into laughter.

Millie shook her head and swallowed. "Amy, you have a heart of gold, and I'd sure like to believe that every single person here understands that." She looked squarely at me, and I let out a ragged sigh.

How could this woman roll out of the hospital and already be alert enough to start up her shenanigans again?

I held up my empty beer bottle. "We all do, Millie. We all do."

Millie went back to chatting with Grace and Nina, another granddaughter, who'd just arrived when Amy's eyes locked on mine. I glanced at my phone, thinking I should head out soon. I'd only had one beer and in another thirty minutes, I should be fine.

But with the way Millie kept looking at me, I couldn't afford to stay much longer.

"You know, I have to confess something," she said softly as her sister and her boyfriend wandered toward the kitchen.

My heart skipped a beat, but I straightened.

"What's that?"

Her nose wrinkled in a cute way as she looked around

117

the room. "I could get used to living here, but I'm concerned that I might be…"

She stopped.

"Might be what?"

"Nothing." She shook her head and moved her hand along my arm.

Sparks shot through me from her touch. I wondered if she felt them, too, when she kept her gaze away from me.

"Go on," I prompted.

She turned and looked at me. "Do you realize this is the longest conversation we've had?"

"No, I think the conversation back at the office was longer," I teased.

Amy folded her arms across her chest. "No, I'm serious. I feel like I scare you away."

"Scare me away?" I laughed. "Why would you think that?"

"Because the moment I come around, you find a reason to take off or push me out the door."

I scowled. "That's not true."

"It is, and I don't get it. I'm not contagious, and you're going to keep running into me whether you like it or not."

"I don't dislike it."

A knot of tension tightened in my chest right behind my ribcage. Had I been that obvious? It wasn't like I could tell her she turned me on, and in turn, I needed to speed down the highway in the opposite direction for both our sakes.

She stared at me.

"I don't dislike *you*," I tried again.

"Then, what is it?"

I'd thought about Amy from every single angle—sideways, upside down, right-side up.

Every single direction pointed to the obvious.

I'd hurt her because I couldn't commit to her.

I couldn't commit to anyone.

So, the best thing for me to do was to avoid her.

I'd just get better at it.

"I have a lot on my mind."

She nodded, not looking like she believed me at all. "Escaped mules and all?"

I chuckled and rocked back on my heels. "It's a little more than that. I do actually tend to some pretty serious things from time to time."

Amy nodded but didn't take her eyes away from me. "I don't doubt it."

"So, you said you could get used to living here, but you're concerned you might be...?"

119

Her right brow arched, and she let out a deep breath. "That I might be overlooking something obvious right in front of me."

"Like what?"

Amy pressed her teeth into her lip, and the fragile skin paled as her teeth ground harder into the usually pink flesh.

She shrugged. "Nothing. It's silly."

It felt like someone was watching us. I glanced over at Millie, who pretended to be looking for something in her purse.

My thumb instinctively swept under Amy's chin as I tipped her head up and lowered my voice. "Nothing you could say would be silly."

"It probably won't make any sense."

"I'm extremely well-versed in the nonsensical."

She chuckled, and I wished I could pull more of the sound out of her. "I grew up in a small town. It was nothing like this one."

I nodded. "There are very few places like Buttercup Lake."

She slid her tongue along her bottom lip as she contemplated what to say. "I'm scared one day, I'll wake up and feel trapped, and everything about this place was a ruse. That I didn't find my home after all."

Her words gutted me. "You're trying to find your home?"

She nodded. "I think so. I think, in truth, I've always been searching for a place to call home. It's why I like nannying. Being involved with families who love their kiddos and dote over them has always given me a sense of home and family, even though it wasn't exactly mine." She glanced around the room and brought her arms up to hug herself. "I probably sound like a crazy stalker who's following families around the country." She laughed and shook her head.

"Not at all."

"Anyway, I never thought I'd want to leave Chicago, but I find myself loving so much about this town, and the people…" She grinned. "Apart from you…" Her brows rose. "Have been very welcoming."

I laughed, tipping my head up.

Her fingers swept across my hand. The softness took my breath away as I brought my eyes back to hers.

"I'll work doubly hard to let you know you're welcome here, Amy." I drew a quick breath but let it out slowly, feeling my pulse rattle crazily behind my ears. There was something intoxicating being around Amy, and it was why I always knew I had to make things quick.

"Thank you, Sheriff." She smiled and turned toward

the kitchen, where she met her sister, who was pouring a glass of wine, and I knew now was my time to exit.

By the time I got home, I was mentally exhausted from analyzing everything Amy had said and didn't say. I never would have guessed she'd grown up in a small town. She seemed so put together. Not that the people around Buttercup Lake weren't as put together, but Amy just...

She was different.

That was the problem. Everything about her was unique and alluring, and I wasn't exactly mad at Millie for trying to push us together.

Right before I pulled into my garage, my heart rate spiked when I noticed a large shadow on my porch rounding the bend to the side I couldn't see. It wasn't bear season, and it was far too bulky to be a deer, not to mention it was late into the evening. It had the movements of something more deliberate, like it had been here before.

I glanced around my property and debated whether to call this in.

I'd always loved this wraparound porch, but it wasn't exactly great from a safety perspective. There were several entrances to the house, and most weren't visible from the front.

In Buttercup Lake, it shouldn't matter.

But tonight, it did.

There was definitely someone prowling my home tonight. I thought about the last several guys I'd put behind bars in the county jail, and they were both pretty remorseful on the way in.

That could have changed.

I kept the SUV running and had my hand on my transceiver as I crept my way along the house, looking for any sign to tip me off.

A crash echoed into the air, and my pulse raced as I dashed to see the culprit staring right at me. Her dark eyes were barely visible as a guttural groan left her lips.

I couldn't help but laugh as all the tension left my body.

"Ah, Lucky. You really are an escape artist."

Chapter Eleven

Amy

I spotted Millie all bundled up, staring out the window from the community center as the parade marched down the street in her honor. The red, white, and blue sirens chirped from the patrol cars, and the high school marching band kept a beat of its own while the cheerleaders clapped their hands in tempo.

Izzy and her business club waved colorful signs as her great-grandma looked on proudly.

Only in Wisconsin would you have a parade in the middle of winter, with the cheerleaders bundled up in faux fur and fleece-lined leggings, all with a smile and to show appreciation.

I thought back to what I'd told Nate last night, and it

was true.

I was afraid.

I was afraid that I was missing something here, that this place was too good to be true and the reality of Buttercup Lake would come tumbling down to disappoint me.

And when that happened, I'd be trapped.

I remember the feeling of being suffocated back in my hometown... like I couldn't make it to eighteen fast enough. There were days when I woke up in high school and worried I'd never leave and turn out like my parents.

I wished for all the things they were too terrified to achieve.

A shudder ran through me as my sister bounded up behind me, crunching on homemade granola.

"This is the best I've ever tasted. I've already ordered three bags of it to take back to Chicago."

"On the plane? How's that going to work?"

She laughed and shook her head. "No. George is driving us back. I do not want to experience a flight like that again."

I chuckled. "Oh, come on. The sun is shining, and the temperature is gonna hit mid-thirties tomorrow."

It wasn't like she wasn't used to frigid temps back in Illinois. We both were, and we happened to enjoy the iciness of the winter and the balminess of spring.

"You were right," my sister whispered.

"About what?"

"This place is alright." She waited for my reaction, but I had none.

This was precisely what worried me here. It was as if there were something in the water that could turn people's pessimism into optimism and cynicism into hope.

"Yeah, but there has to be something more going on." I shook my head as a tractor with streamers went by.

"No, don't let my orneriness sway you. It's good people here. Seriously. This place is nothing like back home where we grew up."

I chuckled. "We'll see."

Right when I turned my attention back to the parade, I saw Sheriff Nate bringing up the end of the parade with a mule wearing a colorful blanket with the word "Lucky" crocheted into a giant scarf.

"Is that who I think it is?" Alice asked, looking over at me.

"Yeah, and is that the mule?"

"Sure is," I said, laughing.

Zipping my coat, I turned and darted out of the community center to see Nate and Lucky coming into the parking lot.

"Is that the culprit?" I called as people started filing into the community center.

Nate's gaze found me as I made my way over to a trailer that he was loading Lucky into.

"She sure is," he said, scratching her neck. "She's the one who got me in all sorts of trouble. Aren't you, girl?"

I stared at Nate, realizing I'd never seen this side before.

"You do have a heart," I teased.

"Hey, what's that supposed to mean?"

I flashed a grin in his direction. "I don't know. You just seem all business, all the time."

"Well, maybe that's because we've only had business with each other."

I shook my head. "Nope. I met you at the holiday party at Hunter's and you barely looked in my direction, and there were no criminals present. Can I pet her?"

"Go for it," he said as I moved next to him and let my fingers tangle in Lucky's mane. She moved her neck slightly so she could see me, and I smiled.

"Did you name her Lucky because you got to see me naked thanks to her?" I asked, smiling and taking a step back.

Nate started laughing and shook his head. "Uh, no.

My mom named her."

I burst into laughter and shook my head. "Sorry about that."

"No need to apologize. It's a good guess."

"So, we're both on the same page with what happened."

His brows rose, and I saw a flicker of heat dart through his gaze. "You mean what I did or didn't see?"

I nodded, feeling a flutter in my stomach the moment his eyes fastened back onto mine.

He didn't answer. Instead, he glanced around the parking lot as more people filed into the community center.

"You've done a good thing here, Amy."

Would I ever get over the thrill of hearing my name roll off his tongue?

"Millie doesn't like attention like this, but I think she needed to see how much she does for this town."

I nodded, shoving my gloved hands into my pockets. "She's an amazing gal, and she always seems to be working behind the scenes on so many things. Did you know she's the one who oversees the giving tree in the lobby here and that she delivers meals to veterans on the weekends?"

Nate's smile only widened. "I did."

"And whether it's true or not about the matchmaking

gig, I think she's such a great example of what a woman in a small town can accomplish."

Nate's eyes didn't stray from mine. "So, you're not completely against small towns."

I pushed down a swallow of nerves that suddenly emerged and didn't answer. The guy was just too attractive for his own good.

"You know, sometimes, I'd like to hear about the small town you grew up in." He watched me closely as I drew a breath and nodded, knowing it wasn't a place I liked to think about.

He seemed to catch that and nodded.

"Or I could tell you about growing up here," he offered, smiling. "Either way, I'd like to prove to you that I'm not running away from you."

I couldn't help the smile that was spreading over me as I stared at the sheriff.

"I'd like that."

"So would I." He ushered Lucky into her area of the trailer and closed up the tail end. "I need to deliver Lucky back to my parents."

"Oh, right. It was nice to meet her."

"I'm sure she feels the same." Nate stopped in front of me before walking to the truck's cab. "Do you mind if I call you on the number you gave me the other day?"

I chuckled and shook my head. "I knew that was how you asked women out."

He laughed and shook his head. "Believe it or not, you're the first."

"I'm not sure I am, but yeah. Call me on that number."

His smile widened, and I suddenly wished he didn't have to go.

Nate looked over my shoulder and brought his gaze back to me. "Just so you know, there's an audience waiting behind you. They're all peeking out the window."

"You're kidding."

"Nope."

"It would be funny if we gave them something to look at."

"Like what?"

I stepped forward, pretending I was going to kiss him, and he laughed. "You are trouble."

I chuckled, reaching out for his arm. "Maybe a little."

Nate let out a low grumble. "You want to keep them guessing?"

"It might make Millie's day," I offered, feeling giddiness slide through me.

"Well, if you think it's a good idea," he said, lowering

his voice. He slowly stepped forward.

"I think it's a terrible idea," I said softly, looking into his hazel eyes. "But I can't stop myself from pretending a little."

I took a step toward Nate, and he looped his arm around my waist, pulling me closer, but not close enough.

From their vantage point, it probably looked like I was in his arms, bodies pressing against one another…

I looked into his eyes and smiled. "Now what?"

His eyes fell to my mouth, and heat pooled in my belly. He leaned closer, tipped his head, and parted his lips slowly.

"I'll see you around sometime, Amy." He loosened his embrace and took a step back, leaving me in a flurry of pent-up desire.

Nate walked to the front of his truck, looking sexy without even trying as his uniform clung to his thin hips and thick thighs.

I spun around, spotting the audience he was referring to, and smiled as I walked to the entrance of the community center.

By the time I opened the door, they'd scattered like rats. I spotted Millie pretending like she was interested in her cuticles, Izzy staring at her own poster, and my sister still eating granola like it was popcorn.

"How was it?" she asked as I made my way over.

"How was what?" I feigned innocence.

"The kiss."

I shook my head and laughed. "We didn't kiss."

"Millie said she saw tongue."

I burst into laughter. "Fifty feet across a parking lot?"

"Are you going to call her a liar after everything she's been through?" my sister teased.

"Not even a little one," I whispered, trying to shake the feelings washing over me.

Nate's mouth had been inches away. His lips never touched mine, but they were left tingling with some sort of craving I didn't understand.

I wiped my fingertips along my mouth and shook my head, relishing in the numbness along my lips. Maybe it was frostbite and had nothing to do with the anticipation sweeping up between Nate and me.

That had to be it.

"What are you doing? Wiping away evidence?" My sister waggled her brows.

"It's not like Nate was wearing lipstick." I grinned, thinking back to the look in his eyes.

Maybe he didn't mind me, after all.

Or he was a showman. I let out a disgruntled sigh. That was probably what happened, the way my picker usually landed.

"I just wanted to give Millie a little extra satisfaction today. That's all."

"Okay. If you say so. Want some granola?" my sister asked, shoving an open bag in front of me.

"You know what? I would. Thanks." I took the bag from my sister and saw so many people coming up to Millie to wish her well.

It made my heart truly happy.

This event had turned out even better than I'd hoped. When I'd planned this, I hadn't even expected her to be well enough to participate, and here she was, getting to enjoy and see what she meant to the town.

But I couldn't stop thinking about the growing crush I had on Nate. It was worrisome because something was bound to happen to ruin it.

As we roamed down an aisle, I saw a rack full of colorful crocheted bikinis.

"You don't see that every day in the middle of Wisconsin," I teased, glancing at my sister.

We both wandered over, and I immediately picked up a pink crocheted bandeau top and boy brief bottom. I never in a million years imagined how cute something like this could be.

A woman stood from her stool and walked over. "A lot of women have been buying the sets as lingerie, too. A cute play on lace. Just pair it up with some fuzzy boots, and you'll look like a ski bunny."

"A very cold ski bunny," my sister whispered to her boyfriend.

I held up the pink set and smiled. "I don't have anyone to wear lingerie for, but I can definitely see myself in our backyard this summer with it." *Obviously, not when Brielle and Nick are in town*, I muttered internally.

Out of nowhere, Nate somehow darted into my mind as I paid for my pink bikini, but I quickly shoved him right back out.

Sure, I thought he was cute—okay, downright sexy—but everything about my life here was temporary, and if my choice of men told me anything, it was that I was lousy at choosing them. Being attracted to Nate didn't bode well for the guy. There had to be something wrong with him. Although he was an officer of the law.

I shook my head and clutched my bag. How could he truly be a problem?

As I followed my sister to the next booth, I saw

myself in the mirror. With all the running around this morning to get ready for the parade and bazaar, I didn't realize I looked like my hair got stuck in a freak winter tornado.

My hair color had always been a source of annoyance. Even it couldn't make up its mind. Did it want to be dark blonde, or did it want to be light auburn? Instead, it was a fuzzy mess of both, depending on the lighting.

But the whole hot-mess look I had going on didn't exactly make my confidence soar knowing I'd just almost kissed Nate.

I stopped and looked around the room, seeing the sea of people enjoying baked goods, crafts, and enjoying everyone's company, and it felt good to make use of a small town like this for such a good cause.

"Amy." I heard Millie behind me and turned around to see the older woman making her way toward me. It was hard to believe she'd been in the hospital this week.

"Hi, Millie." I smiled and gave her a hug.

"You really didn't have to go to all this trouble for me."

"I just came up with the idea. The town did the rest. We love you, Millie, and you do so much good."

"We all do," she said, smiling and taking my hand in hers as my sister and boyfriend trundled away. "But there's something special about you."

I shook my head and chuckled softly. "I don't know about that, but thank you."

"It's true." She looked around the room. "And I'm going to tell you something I've never told a soul before."

"What's that?"

"The Sunshine Breakfast Club isn't just a book club."

I feigned innocence. "No way."

She nodded. "Without ever saying a word, we've managed to play Cupid many times over."

"I never would have guessed," I said, trying to keep my face expressionless.

"It's true." She nodded. "All I've ever wanted to do with this little book club is spread a smidge of love wherever I can, and if the two people take the hint and run with it? Even better. But I see that in you, Amy. I think if you kept your eyes peeled, you could spot the potential for love to blossom, too. After all, I merely get a feeling when I see the possibility." She winked at me. "And then I just see what can happen."

"There has to be more to it."

"Well, there's some quick analyzing about personality traits, quirks, and looks, but…" She nodded. "You get the idea. Anyway, when I was sitting in the hospital bed, I realized the one thing I wanted to make sure happened would happen."

"And what's that?"

She squeezed my hands and pulled them to her chest. "That you give Nate a chance. He's a little rough around the edges, and he might seem disinterested, but..." Millie smiled and nodded. "He's got a good heart."

I nodded. "I believe you."

"He just carries something with him that I don't know whether he'll ever truly forgive himself for and... it's kept him from trusting himself."

I looked into Millie's eyes, and I knew she wouldn't lead me astray.

But if he couldn't forgive himself or open up to love, my picker was still as broken as ever because I could easily fall for the sheriff.

Chapter Twelve

Nate

"Is there a reason you're extra ornery this morning, or is it just because the coffee pot is empty?" Jeff asked, adding grounds to the basket. He was one of our newer deputies.

"Am I?" I growled before I started laughing. "Sorry. I'm just… exhausted, but it's no excuse."

"Did you have a busy night last night? I didn't think you were on-call."

"No. It wasn't that."

I couldn't get Amy out of my head, but I certainly wasn't going to say that.

But that was the truth. I just lay in bed, tossing and turning, as I thought about the electricity that I felt being so close to her.

It was on fire.

She was on fire.

That pretend kiss was the undoing of me. We didn't even touch.

It was air!

I think what was worse or better, depending on how I wanted to look at it, was that I finally *felt* something. Truly, deep into my bones, I felt a rise and fall of something I hadn't felt in years.

I'd done such a tremendous job of dulling my emotions since everything happened over ten years ago that I wasn't even sure what to do with the feelings running through me.

"Just didn't sleep well, and I needed some java. Sorry about that."

"Nah. It's no biggie. I'm just used to you joking around and stuff," the officer said, holding his travel mug in the air. "I'll see ya around."

"Sure will." I nodded and let out a deep breath the moment he'd left the breakroom.

One thing was certain. I needed to get ahold of myself.

I walked down the short hallway, waved at Flo, who was busy reading at her desk, then went into my office and closed the door.

I just needed a few minutes, and then I'd be back to normal. Being attracted to a woman didn't mean I had to get down on one knee. I sat at my desk, spinning in my chair to stare at the wall next to me with maps of the area pinned with notes. A relic left over from my uncle. I smiled at the thought. Now, all we had to do was punch a few words into our phone, and an entire GPS system popped up. It would blow his mind.

Letting out a sigh, I wiggled my mouse and stared at my inbox. I'd always prided myself on being rational. I embraced logic and rarely jumped to conclusions that weren't based on some sort of fact or calculated with precise reasoning. I moved my palms over my face and let out a groan.

Yet, here I was, at the mercy of something that wasn't based on logic or facts. It was based on emotions, and that was the one thing I'd managed to stomp down over the years.

I wouldn't say I was emotionless, but I knew how to keep those feelings buried deep to avoid turmoil and needless worry, but whenever I merely bumped into Amy or thought about her, all I wanted to do was run toward her.

Find out about her.

Learn what makes her happy.

Yet, all she'd experienced from me was a man who wanted to run in the other direction to keep her safe and protected and to keep me sane. She didn't know any of that, and that was fine.

Good, actually.

The less time we spent together, the better.

But she was slowly seeping into my world, and I was worried that before I knew it, she'd become the epicenter of my existence.

Everything about her screamed perfection to me, or at least my kind of perfection. Her intelligence was so sexy, with a mind that turned mundane ideas into something sparkly and new with a quick joke or a flutter of her lashes.

And her laughter... It was infectious and haunting in a deliriously wonderful way. There had been a few times when I swore I heard her laughter echoing through my halls at home. But it was like just having her there for a few minutes left an essence of something...

Of her.

I closed my eyes and groaned as I rested my forehead on my fists. I was losing it.

There was no way I was going to call her. It didn't matter that I implied we'd go on a date. I just couldn't risk it. I couldn't play with her heart.

Amy was the most compassionate woman I'd ever met and could light up the darkness in the world with just one smile, but I didn't want to be the one who placed the darkness in her world. She didn't deserve to see me when I had a bad day.

Shoot. Even one of my officers could tell if I was having a bad day, and that was just from grabbing a cup of coffee.

All I knew was that I needed to stay focused and let Amy be Amy without contaminating her spirit. She deserved that from me.

It didn't help that the anniversary of the accident was coming up next week, right before St. Patrick's Day.

Damn, I hated this time of year.

I cleared my throat and straightened in my chair. Today was going to be a day out and about in the community. The fog in my head would only leave if I quit focusing on myself and got out there.

As I scrolled through several emails, I froze at the sight of one.

My best friend from high school, the guy I thought would be by my side for years to come but had to leave after what happened.

I didn't blame him. I couldn't blame him after what took place.

How would he be able to look me in the eyes again

after that night?

Tears pricked my eyes, and I quickly brushed them away.

I had not heard from Tom in over a decade, and I respected his wishes not to contact him or his immediate family.

But I understood.

I understood more fully than he could ever know.

Instead of clicking on the email, I stood up and grabbed my jacket. It was time to get downtown and patrol Buttercup Lake.

That was what I was hired to do many years ago, and recently, that was what I'd been elected to do as sheriff. I couldn't let my personal life color my views of the town and the people I'd been chosen to protect.

I shut off my computer and harnessed up before leaving my office, grabbing my tablet for the vehicle.

Flo looked up at me and smiled. "You look like hell, Sheriff."

I tipped my cowboy hat at her and grinned. "Thanks for that, Flo."

She laughed. "Anytime."

I walked outside to my patrol SUV and climbed in, anchoring my tablet into the dash. It was chilly, but the sunshine was blazing through the brilliant blue sky. Days like this made me love Wisconsin even more. I'd always enjoyed the snow and cold weather, but there was something about seeing the sparkly blue skies cast down over Buttercup Lake that made me certain I'd never leave the town I'd grown up in.

Turning onto Main Street, I thought back to Amy.

Because, of course, I did. I couldn't get her out of my mind. The comments she'd made about the small town she'd grown up in made me curious. I wanted to know more. The idea of her not having an incredible childhood hurt my soul, and I didn't even understand why. She just deserved everything in this world and more, and I wasn't sure she realized it.

I put my blinker on and turned into the public parking area for Buttercup Lake access. They were dotted along the water, but this one had easy access for walking downtown.

It was crazy how much this town grew over the years. Now, it was more of a tourist destination than anything, which was great for our local economy. I pulled into a parking space and climbed out of my vehicle, scanning the frozen lake dotted with fishing huts. If the temperatures stayed like today, there wouldn't be much more ice-fishing this year.

Of course, we'd always have the guys who didn't

want to listen and still set up shop on the ice, only to have the fire department and rescue teams pulling them out of the frigid water when they fell through. I glanced both ways and crossed the street. That always got me. We were here for emergencies and accidents. Public servants wanted to help, but I never understood the philosophy of some people who disregard common sense, do something completely dumb, and then put all the first responders in jeopardy.

Just last year, when we'd specifically posted not to go out on the ice, we had a father and son drill their hole, warm their hands and feet in their tent, and in less than an hour, we were out there pulling them from the slush and ice of the lake. We almost lost a K-9 over it. Thoughtless was what that was.

Amy didn't strike me as someone thoughtless.

Darn it. She crept back in again.

I walked over to the coffee shop and opened the door to see Millie in the corner with her granddaughters and Abby behind the counter.

"Hey, Sheriff. Fancy seeing you here." Abby held up an empty cup. "Your usual?"

"Let's change it up today. I'm feeling—"

"Frisky?" Millie interrupted. "Are you feeling frisky?"

I chuckled and shook my head. "It's good to have you

back in town, Millie. You gave us quite the scare."

"You can't get rid of me that easily." Millie took a bite of a croissant and smiled at me. "Seen Amy today?"

"It's nine o'clock in the morning, Millie. I haven't had much chance for much."

"So, you didn't…"

Grace chuckled. "Grandma, honestly. You're going to get us arrested."

"What would the charge be?" Millie teased. "Making a policeman blush?"

"I'm not blushing, Millie. And I'm not feeling frisky." I grinned, turning my attention back to Abby. "How about a large Americano with ice?"

"Sure thing. A large, iced Americano coming up."

"How come it sounds so much more organized when you say it?"

"Coffee. It's what I do." She winked at me as I wandered down the counter to wait for my drink.

I glanced at Millie and her granddaughters. They looked like they were conspiring. My only hope was that it wasn't about me. A family stared through the window as they debated about coming inside when the woman nodded, and the man opened the door to let their kids inside.

My stomach clenched, and an odd thought occurred

to me.

Would that ever be me?

The kids found a place to sit while their parents went up to the counter to order just as Abby called out my drink. I took it and thanked her as I headed to the door when a disheveled guy burst through, looking a little sloppy for this early in the morning. His jeans hung low, and he didn't really look dressed for a Wisconsin winter in his light jacket. He refused eye contact with me as he brushed past me, which made me do a double-take and decide to stay indoors and drink my iced Americano.

Abby glanced at me nervously as the man appeared to pace a few steps back and forth before moving toward the counter. We'd have robberies here once in a blue moon, but it never hurt to be cautious. I took a seat near the door and watched the man fumble in his pocket. He pulled out a worn wallet and looked up at Abby.

"Hey, Sir. Can I get a drink started for you?"

"I just wanted a water and a muffin."

"Sure thing." She nodded, giving me a relieved look as she reached in the glass cabinet for the muffin.

As she served him the muffin, he handed her cash and then glanced around before leaning over the counter and slipping out a picture.

"Have you seen her?" he asked. "I heard she's living here now, and I'd love to surprise her. We grew up together."

A flicker of recognition darted through Abby's gaze, but she shook her head. "No, I haven't seen anyone like her, but I'll keep my eyes out. You're in town for a while?"

His shoulders slouched, and he nodded. "Oh, okay. Yeah. For a little bit."

Abby slid a cup of water to him. "Where are you from?"

"You've never heard of it. Just a small town outside of Oklahoma."

"Oh. Well, I hope you enjoy your visit here. I hope you can find your friend."

"Me too," he mumbled and grabbed his food and water before he headed out the door, wandering down the sidewalk.

"Who's he looking for?" I asked, walking over to Abby. "I could tell you recognized whoever was in the photo."

She nodded and drew a deep breath. "I did. It was a picture of Amy."

Chapter Thirteen

Amy

Tate had just eaten a plate of strawberries and seemed extremely content sleeping on a blanket on the floor in the family room. One minute, he was playing. The next, he was sawing logs from all the excitement. He was so darling, and today was no different. Daisy had dressed him up in a sailor outfit, and his baby pudge squeezed through his sleeves, begging to be tickled.

I sat next to him on the floor, leaning against the couch, and reached for my phone. My sister had left last weekend, and Brielle and Nick had touched down briefly— just long enough to pack and give me a list of everything they needed me to do while they were gone. Brielle had full intentions of coming back every couple of weeks, and I suppose when money was no object, it wasn't a crazy idea.

A call came over my cellphone with a number I didn't recognize but with an area code from my hometown. I froze, worried something had happened to my parents, and slid my phone on.

"This is Amy," I said, nearly whispering so I didn't wake up Tate.

I stood up and slowly made my way to the kitchen.

"Amy, it's Leo."

My blood turned icy as heat crept up my spine. "How'd you get my number?"

"Your mom gave it to me. Said you were doing really well working for some ultra-rich folks."

My pulse hammered as the room turned around me. It felt like I'd gotten thrown back to another time and place as dread threaded through me.

"It's not quite like that," I said, feeling my mouth turn extremely dry.

"I need to see you," he said suddenly.

"I—uh." The words refused to come. "I can't leave right now, Leo."

"You don't have to. I'm here in town." He laughed, but it wasn't a sound I recognized from him. This tone sounded distant and... strange. "You're in Wisconsin, right?"

"Leo, I can't. I'm sorry."

"Oh, come on, Ames. I used my last few dollars to get here and find this dump of a hotel to stay in. Your mom said those people aren't in town. Won't you let me crash there while I figure things out?"

Everything in my world that I'd tried so hard to escape from was crumbling on top of me at this moment, pulling me right into the suffocating world of small-town problems I'd vowed to escape.

"I can't. It's not my home to offer," I said softly. "Leo, this isn't a good idea."

"Too late, Ames. I'm already in town."

I cringed at his nickname for me. Growing up, it was innocent and cute, but it became anything but as time went on. The last time he'd called me Ames, he'd been pleading for help.

Help that I'd long since realized I couldn't give him.

"What? You don't want your friends to know about me? Do I embarrass you?" His laughter pricked my spine as I looked over at little Tate.

His innocence.

I shut my eyes and let out a deep breath, grateful I was at Hunter and Daisy's today while they were at Hunter's new restaurant. If my mom had given him Brielle's address, at least

I wasn't there.

"It's not that, Leo. But I can't. Please respect my wishes and go back home."

He laughed. "Home? I don't have a home, Ames. You know that. Neither of us did."

"I can't help you, Leo. You know that. I need to go."

I hung up the phone with trembling hands and slid onto the kitchen floor with my head in my hands as I realized no matter how hard I tried, I couldn't escape the past that tried to pull me down.

I felt caught in the tide of uncertainty as two of my worlds threatened to collide. My mom knew I never wanted Leo to know where I was or what I was doing, and yet she told him everything and embellished even more.

There was nothing more I could do but hope Leo would leave. I pulled myself off the floor and poured myself a cup of coffee, drinking it with my hands still shaking.

I wasn't embarrassed by Leo. I was scared of what he represented. It could have been me or my sister, but we beat the odds and left, and I just never expected that place to come find me. He was the place.

But it was almost like the universe was reminding me why I couldn't fall for the allure of small towns, specifically, Buttercup Lake.

Why I couldn't fall for the sheriff.

Nate had no plans of leaving, and I certainly wasn't going to be staying.

Leo's call reminded me of that quite well. I needed a wide, vast city where I could just disappear and let my destiny flourish without the trappings of small-town living.

Families had lived in my hometown for generations, and it took so much to push through the guilt of wanting more than my parents had been content with. I never wanted to appear ungrateful or make it look like I was turning my back on the community that helped raise me, but it would be a lie. There were very few people in that town who ever worried about Alice or me, and I finally realized it was fear that nearly held me back. I was afraid of failing, of discovering that I wasn't equipped for the world outside my small town. The thought was an almost paralyzing fear fraught with the worry and shame that would accompany me if I had to return, not for a visit, but for a lifetime.

But the last night I was with Leo told me everything. I had to leave. I needed to defy the odds and listen to the tiny spark of hope that refused to extinguish and follow my heart into the adulthood I created.

Yet, just picking up the phone and hearing Leo's voice trampled over everything I'd accomplished, everything

I'd left behind.

I walked over to little Tate, who hadn't stirred one bit, other than a little upturn of his lips as happy dreams floated through his little mind. It was moments like these when I knew I'd made the right choice to leave. These moments also reminded me how much I wanted to be a mom someday.

I just didn't know if that was in the cards.

My phone buzzed, and I nearly jumped on the couch. It was a local number and the text read,

You home? I'd like to swing by.

I shook my head. Oh, no. Did Leo steal someone's phone?

It's business, not personal.

It was like all the tension released from my body at once, and I didn't feel so alone any longer. I quickly texted to come on by to Daisy and Hunter's, but to knock lightly since Tate was napping.

I sat down next to Tate and smiled as he started to rouse. He tended to wiggle a little while sleeping and then sleep some more.

Only a few minutes had passed when I heard a light tap and received a text from Nate. I looked at Tate and pushed myself off the ground to answer the door.

With each step closer, an unexpected lightness filled me. I had no intentions of telling the sheriff about my unexpected visitor, but just having him here made me feel… lighter.

I opened the door and smiled. "Where's your cowboy hat, Sheriff?"

"I thought I could leave it in the vehicle this time, Amy." He looked over my shoulder. "Alright if I come inside?"

"Absolutely. Tate is napping on the floor. It was a bit impromptu. One minute, he was playing with blocks, and the next, he was snoozing."

Nate's eyes stayed fastened on mine while I shut the door behind him. "You really love what you do, don't you?"

I nodded, feeling the familiar warmth spread through me. There was something about the way he looked at me that just made me feel like things would be okay.

It was probably all the years of training and police work.

"Would you like a cup of coffee or anything?"

"No, I won't be long. I just wanted to stop by and

see…" He kept his eyes locked on me. "Well, not that it's my business, but I happened to be at the coffee shop this morning, and a man came in looking for you."

The life that I'd meticulously built piece by piece away from the town that raised me was shattering like a mosaic tossed into the fragile streets of Buttercup Lake. I'd created a delicate balance of old and new, focusing on my future. Never in a million years did I think my past would come back like this. Not here.

"Everything okay, Amy?" Nate asked, taking a step closer.

I nodded. "Sorry. No, I just… right before you texted, I got a call from someone I thought…"

Nate looked at me with patience and concern in his eyes, but he didn't press.

I looked into the family room to see Tate still snoozing as I let out a deep breath.

"I'm guessing it was Leo."

His brows raised. "Leo? An old boyfriend?"

My cheeks flushed. "It's a long story. Complicated."

"I see." He nodded, glancing toward the family room. "Did you want to tell me about it?"

"Maybe someday," I said softly.

A few seconds of silence lingered between us.

"Do you mind that he's looking for you? Abby said she didn't recognize you. We weren't sure of your thoughts on the matter."

I noticed his jaw clench as he studied me closely.

"I appreciate that. I'm just so sorry my problems followed me here."

Nate nodded and folded his hands. "I understand that."

"This is all so unexpected and embarrassing and..."

"You have nothing to be embarrassed about, Amy. We all have our pasts and things we wished worked out in different ways or maybe never happened at all."

I nodded.

"Is he part of the reason you're not fond of small towns?" he asked.

"He pretty much put the nail in the coffin on that one. Yeah." I shook my head. "But probably not how you think."

Nate's hazel eyes showed nothing but kindness, no judgment.

Just kindness.

"Well, I wanted you to be aware that this man is wandering around town looking for you, and it sounds like you might not want to be found."

"You could say that." I shrugged. "But it is what it

is."

"Are you afraid for your safety?" Nate's expression turned serious as darkness drifted behind his gaze.

I shook my head. "No. I don't think so."

"The answer to that question should always be no, Amy."

I swallowed down my embarrassment, knowing he was absolutely right.

"I can put a few more officers on this route, if you'd like. There's not much more I can do other than that until you want to tell me more."

"You don't have to do that."

"Amy, I want to."

"Thank you, Sheriff." I nodded, crossing my arms over my chest. "That was a chapter in my life that I never expected to reopen."

"Understood. If you need anything..." Nate glanced into the family room. "Anything at all, you have my number now. Use it."

"I'm sorry about this," I muttered as he started toward the door.

Nate stopped so suddenly that I crashed into his back. He turned around even though we were nearly on top of each other and shook his head.

"You don't have anything to apologize for, Amy."

I looked up into his eyes, feeling his towering presence comfort me, and it suddenly became hard to breathe.

His eyes swept my mouth before bringing his gaze back to mine. "I'm a good listener too."

I nodded. "I'll keep that in mind."

"You said his name was Leo?"

"Yeah."

"Leo from Oklahoma," he muttered, walking to the door.

"I never told you I was from Oklahoma."

He looked over his shoulder and opened the door. "No, but he did at the coffee shop, and I intend to find out more."

And just like that, two worlds I'd fought to keep separate for so long were suddenly twisting together into an endless vine of past, present, and future that threatened to take my dreams away.

Chapter Fourteen

Nate

Amy had clearly been uncomfortable, and I never intended for that to happen, but I needed to know if she wanted to be found by this guy, and it was safe to say the answer was a resounding *no*.

The problem was that we lived in a town filled with people who were overwhelmingly helpful, especially to visitors.

Amy's response to my questions were firm, yet thoughtful. She didn't want to say too much to give anything away. That I gathered quickly. I also heard the thread of self-preservation weave through Amy's words, and I finally realized she'd built her world like a fortress. She didn't just leave the small town behind to dream big. She did it to safeguard her own future, to protect herself from the chaos of her past.

And with everything in me, I wanted to know what built that chaos, what brought Leo to town looking for her.

I stood in my kitchen and opened a beer. I certainly didn't want to misinterpret the signs Amy gave me, but I couldn't help but meticulously examine the clues for the rest of the day. Each glance she gave me, each shudder of her body, told me that she didn't want to see this guy again.

But I could tell by the determination in Leo's eyes that he wasn't going to leave Buttercup Lake until he found her.

Why?

That was the million-dollar question that worried me.

Really worried me.

The one thing I caught in Amy's gaze was doubt, and what troubled me was that I didn't know if she was doubting me or herself.

Or was she doubting Leo?

Doubt always managed to be a persistent opponent, especially when it came to believing your own intuition, and I saw that struggle in Amy today.

I replayed our interactions repeatedly today, and everything pointed to protection.

Amy needed protection, but I didn't know if it was

more from Leo or from herself. She looked so defeated, and it was unlike anything I'd ever seen from Amy. She always seemed so approachable and unstoppable, and today, I caught a hint of uncertainty and loneliness.

I wanted her to open up to me, but there wasn't anything I could do. We weren't there yet in our relationship, friendship or otherwise, to have her confide in me.

But one thing I knew. At some point, she'd loved Leo. I didn't know what kind of love, but it was there. I saw the pain from it stretching her heart, threatening to tear it apart just from knowing he was around.

And that killed me.

It wasn't that I didn't expect Amy to have had feelings for a man before, but what I saw in her eyes was different. It was heavy and filled with a history I didn't understand, and I might never.

I'd been wrestling with the vision of Leo and who I thought Amy would go for, and he was anything but it, and it made me wonder if everything I'd been contemplating was fruitless, anyway. Leo struck me as my complete opposite in all ways.

The gnawing sensation nipping at me only grew this evening, and I had to find out more, one way or another.

I opened my laptop and continued my pursuit of

information. I'd found out which small town Amy had grown up in, and it answered a lot of questions. The crime rate was off the charts, and the drug problems had grown exponentially during her youth there, and I'd also narrowed down the Leonards in her age range. A slight amount of trepidation filled me as I continued scanning for information. Amy probably wouldn't be happy if she knew I was sniffing around her past, but I wasn't focused on finding out anything about her. I was only determined to learn more about the man coming here to see her.

A ruckus out back caught my attention, so I closed the lid of the laptop and flipped on the back porch light to see Lucky nosing around my patio furniture.

"What the hell?" I muttered to myself. I opened the door and whistled. "Lucky, go back home."

She stared at me as if she were home, and I knew looking up Leo intel would have to wait. This was getting crazy.

Absurd, really. Why was this mule infatuated with me?

I slid out my phone, and my dad laughed before I even said my greeting.

"I'm already on my way. Your mom noticed she wasn't in her pen or the stable a few minutes ago."

"Is this normal?"

My dad chuckled. "Define normal."

"Alright, see you soon," I said, hanging up.

I walked back over to my laptop and glanced at Lucky, who'd planted her nose on my glass. With every breath, a puff of condensation steamed up the door surrounding her nostrils. She wasn't going anywhere.

Taking a seat, I lifted the lid and started scanning for the right Leonard. And then—Bam! I'd found him.

Leonard Mitzel. I scribbled down his birthdate and let out a deep breath as I heard my dad's truck backing into the drive.

Walking over to the door, I swung it open and saw my dad pulling on his gloves as he walked over.

"Where's she at?" my dad asked.

"Back porch so she can have a better view of me working."

"I hate to mention this, but you might need to adopt a mule." My dad gripped my shoulder and squeezed it as I welcomed him in.

He made his way down the hall and into the kitchen where Lucky stood on the other side of the glass.

My dad caught the image of Leo on my screen. "Who's that guy? I don't recognize him."

"No, he's not from the area."

"Oh, yeah?" My dad glanced at me. "Then why are you looking him up?"

"Want to take a seat?" I asked, pointing at the kitchen table chairs.

"What the heck. I don't think Lucky's leaving."

I nodded, kicking out my chair. "You know that woman, Amy."

"Yeah, the one you didn't invite for dinner."

"Right. Anyway, that guy came into town looking for her. She wasn't expecting him."

"Didn't want to see him?" my dad asked.

"Didn't seem like it. She wouldn't tell me much, and there's not much I can do unless she does. So I thought in the meantime, I'd look some stuff up."

My dad flashed a wry grin. "Just for fun?"

"I wouldn't call it fun."

"Oh, you live for this type of thing."

I shrugged and let out a deep breath. "Amy just doesn't seem like the type of woman who'd hang out with a guy like that."

"I'm guessing she's not. I mean, she's not with him, right?"

"No, but I sensed a deep history there. I mean, she

didn't say as much, but..." I pressed my lips together and shook my head. "I don't know. I'm sticking my nose where it doesn't belong."

"But she doesn't want to see the guy?"

"No."

A few minutes of silence sat between us as Lucky continued to breathe heavily on the glass.

My dad finally broke the silence with a blend of concern and tenderness. "Whoever this guy is, he's no longer in the picture."

"Correct."

He let out a sigh. "The fact that you're here, looking things up about this guy, talking about this with your old man, and worrying about her, tells me you do care about her."

"I care about all the people who live here." I stared at Leo's photo. His dark, greasy hair and thin frame took up most of the frame.

"But might you care for her in a... different way?" my dad tried again.

"I told you, Dad. I just can't get involved. I'm not cut out for it."

"Probably doesn't help that the anniversary is coming up."

The words turned the air icy as I brought my gaze to

my dad's. "Yeah. It's probably making me think if I couldn't protect Ella, then maybe I can't help Amy."

"And that, Son, is my fear." He shook his head. "You weren't responsible for what happened that night. It was a fluke. Nobody blames you."

"Tom certainly did, and he had every right to."

"Not true, Nate." My dad shook his head. "You weren't to blame for what happened, and it kills me to think you've spent the last decade thinking just that, and in turn, closing your heart off from the world."

"It's not like that, Dad."

"Oh, yeah?" He looked over at Leo's picture. "Then why can't you admit you like Amy?"

"Because no matter how much I don't want to admit it, we all carry our pasts with us. These moments in time are glued fastidiously into our being, cells, thoughts, and memories." I shook my head. "And because of that, I know I can't commit to someone who needs... who is..."

My dad studied me. "Who is what?"

"Who is as compassionate, tender, and loving as Amy. What she did for Millie sealed the deal. I was drawn to her from the moment I saw her, and then when she did all of that for a woman she barely knows..." I couldn't help myself. "I asked her if it was alright if I called her to go out sometime, but by the time I got home, I knew it was a bad idea. I was just caught up in the moment."

"So, you won't allow yourself to date someone who is kind or compassionate?"

I laughed, knowing it would sound ridiculous when said aloud. "It's not like that. It's just that I don't want to destroy Amy."

"You couldn't destroy anyone on your worst day, Nate."

"But what if I can't protect her?"

The words floated in the air, and I knew that was the problem. Years ago, I lost someone who meant so much to me, my best friend, our families. I couldn't protect her. What if I couldn't protect the woman I fell in love with?

"Maybe you came into Amy's life for a simple reason right now. Nothing more. Nothing less."

"What's that reason?"

"To be her safe place. Maybe, you can be the person she turns to when the ghosts of her past finally come out to haunt her. Allow her to feel safe. That is enough." My dad reached over and patted my leg. "Don't overthink things, Son. Sometimes, we just need to feel safe and heard. Let her feel both."

"Quit running from her," I said softly.

"Especially that, if that's what you've been doing."

I nodded. "Yeah. You're right."

My dad stood. "I know I'm right. Now, let's get Lucky back in the truck, yet again, and get her home."

"Sounds good, Dad. And thanks."

"For what?"

"Telling me what I needed to hear tonight."

"It's a rare occasion you or your brother will listen to it." He laughed.

"Not true." My phone buzzed, and I glanced down to see a text from Amy.

"Hey, I got this. My back's better, and there are no ice patches in sight."

"You sure?"

"Absolutely. You take care of business." He stopped at the front door. "And one word of advice. Quit looking up Leo and just ask her. Find out what he's done to her and stop worrying about what he's done to society."

"I wasn't going to run a—"

My dad's brows raised. "You've never made a habit of lying to your dad, so let's not start now."

I chuckled and nodded as my dad wandered out of the house.

Picking up my phone, I opened the message from

Amy, and my heart pounded.

I looked out the window to see my dad already leading Lucky around the house, and I knew my dad had been right.

If nothing else, I could be Amy's safe place, but first, she had to trust me, and I didn't know if I'd be able to break down those walls in time.

Before Leo completely broke her spirit.

Chapter Fifteen

Amy

Tate was with Daisy and Hunter at their home, and they didn't expect to need my services for the next few days, which was a relief. As I sat in their family room while Tate was sleeping, I couldn't help but come to the conclusion that I couldn't watch Tate until after Leo left.

Something Nate said rang true. I should know in my heart whether or not Leo would do something to me.

And the truth of it was that the little boy I grew up with never would, but the man Leo became might. Not because of an evil inside him.

No. I still believed the fun-spirited little boy who would help me collect rocks or spend our days on a swing at the park was inside him, but because of the addiction... that led him down a path I could never have predicted.

I couldn't fathom why he was here in Buttercup Lake, and if he'd spent his last nickel getting here, there was no doubt that his addiction would start directing him to feed the craving, and I certainly wouldn't put little Tate in harm's way.

Hopefully, Leo would just leave and I'd never have to mention things to Daisy and Hunter, because it was downright embarrassing, but I'd never jeopardize Tate. If Leo was still around, I wouldn't feel comfortable watching Tate. I just wouldn't.

Which was what led me to text Nate. When he came over, I could see real concern etching his expression. It was like he knew I needed something, only I didn't even know what that was.

I wanted to tell him when he was in front of me, just let everything fly out of my mouth like there weren't consequences, but I knew better.

No matter how amazing Buttercup Lake was, if I brought trouble to town, why would they forgive me?

And Leo was trouble.

Not necessarily on purpose, but it just seemed to follow him.

To Buttercup Lake.

I poured boiling water over a peppermint tea bag and

bounced it up and down while I waited for Nate. To say I felt sheepish was putting it lightly, but once the sun set, I felt a little… off. Suddenly, these giant windows overlooking the lake didn't feel so cozy. The glass felt prying.

A shiver ran through me, and I let out a deep breath.

Leo was harmless. He just was. I needed to remind myself of that.

But why?

The doorbell rang, and my heart jumped into my throat. I wasn't sure if it was because Nate was on the other side of the door or because I was worried it was Leo.

I pushed my worries aside and walked to the door with my tea in hand. If it were Nate, I'd look more relaxed than I felt. If it was Leo, I could throw it at him.

Not really, but if I had to…

A knock sounded, and I quickened my step. This house was so darn big, it was difficult to get from one area to the next in a timely fashion.

I finally got to the door, straightened, and let out another deep breath.

"Who is it?" I asked.

"The sheriff. I mean Nate."

I chuckled, feeling relief swim through me at a rapid pace. Flinging the door open, I lit up at the sight of him.

Nate wasn't in his uniform. Instead, he wore a slouchy pair of jeans that fit just right at the hips and thighs, looking a little worn along the pocket edges. He'd buttoned a blue plaid flannel over a dark grey Henley. He hadn't even bothered with a coat. The sight of him nearly made me feel like a sloppy, wet noodle, wanting to be slurped up.

"I got here as fast as I could. Lucky was over at my house again, so I had to help get her settled down in the trailer."

My heart skipped a beat at the mere sight of him. "No. Please, don't apologize. Are you kidding? I'm just so grateful you came over. I feel kind of crazy for texting, but…"

His hand unexpectedly touched mine. "Don't. That's what I'm here for, Amy. I meant it."

My cheeks warmed from his words, and I nodded while motioning him inside.

I couldn't help but do a quick peek around the front before closing the door.

"Did you want any tea, wine, water?" I took a sip of my hot tea. "I have food, too. Lots of snacks and things I can prep if you want more."

Nate laughed in a completely disarming way, and the sound was irresistible. "Should I have packed a bag?"

I laughed, shaking my head. "Sorry. No. Not at all."

He smiled, still chuckling. It was the most infectious sound, the deep rumbling that erupted from within, and it was genuine, completely genuine.

And for some reason, it was the one grounding force I needed to hear tonight.

My gaze dropped to my cup of tea as I thought about telling Nate about Leo. Maybe it had been a bad idea. As of now, Nate just knew me as Amy. I was worried about how that would change, but with all the unsettled feelings washing over me, I needed someone.

"How about a glass of wine?" Nate asked. "I'm off duty."

I nodded happily. "Absolutely. Red or white?"

"Red sounds good." Nate came up behind me as I walked into the kitchen, and his energy slammed into me like a freight train.

His presence just commanded attention, and if it had been any other night, I probably would have spun around and accidentally bumped into him for a kiss.

But not tonight, and probably never.

I pulled a wine glass from the cupboard and opened a bottle that I'd bought weeks ago.

"You doing okay?" Nate asked.

Pouring the crimson liquid into the glass, I nodded

and then shook my head. "I don't know. I'm a complete mess."

I handed him the glass, and he smiled. "That's quite the pour."

Chuckling, I nodded. "I know how long you'll be here." I set the bottle on the counter and looked up at Nate. A faint smirk lined his lips, but it wasn't off-putting or arrogant. It was charming and somewhat challenging.

"I'm in no hurry." His eyes stayed on mine as I took a sip of tea. "I will do my best to listen and offer advice or none at all. Whatever you need, Amy."

I focused on Nate. "Really? You mean it?"

Nate nodded.

"I can't thank you enough for coming over. I just don't feel comfortable talking to anyone about this yet, and…" my voice trailed off. "I don't want Daisy or Hunter to think less of me."

His eyes darkened briefly as he took a sip of his wine, but his gaze stayed on mine over the rim.

"The family room is pretty comfortable," I offered, motioning him to follow me.

"Lead the way," he said, following behind.

"Beautiful home Brielle and Nick made for themselves."

"It is." I nodded. "It's a shame they're rarely in it."

"True."

"Personally, I'd love a one-room cabin or an old farmhouse." I turned and pulled a couple of pillows from the couch and sat down, putting them back on my lap. Nate sat next to me a few sections down. He set the wine glass on the coffee table.

I'd turned on the fireplace before he got here because I hadn't been able to shake off the chill that had settled over me the moment I got the call from Leo.

"So, Leo…" he said, pressing his lips into a thin line.

"He's not a bad guy," I said, unable to believe I was already coming to his defense, which was ridiculous. Nate didn't have to be here. I called him over. "He's just a product of…" I stopped myself, looked at Nate, and realized I couldn't say it. As I looked at Nate, it would be a completely hypocritical thing to say.

"A product of a small town?" Nate finished my sentence for me.

I let out a sigh. "I think I'm going to switch to what you're having. I'll be right back."

"Take your time," Nate said softly. "I'm not going anywhere."

I smiled and walked back into the kitchen, almost in

a trance as I realized I'd spent a lifetime blaming all the bad on the town I grew up in, and I used it to make excuses for Leo from the moment he'd started slipping. And those same assertions were about to roll off my lips to an incredible man who was also a product of a small town and who was a better man for it. My grasp on reality shifted into a complicated territory that actually scared me.

Because it gave me, and it gave the individuals living in the town I grew up in, the ability to choose the life we'd forged. That meant some of us chose well and others poorly, but in my heart, I knew it wasn't that simple.

I poured myself an equally large glass of wine and went back into the family room, where Nate was still sitting. His knee bobbed a little as he looked out the floor-to-ceiling windows.

"Sorry about that," I said, sliding back into my place. I tucked my legs under me and turned my attention to Nate. "Liquid courage is at it again."

"Take a sip," he said, chuckling. "I think you might need it more than me."

I chuckled, feeling the unease trickle out of me as I followed his instructions.

"And Amy, there's nothing that you could tell me that would make me think less of you. Nothing."

Bringing my gaze to his, I smiled. "There's something about you that is so disarming."

He looked surprised. "Really? That's not usually something a police officer hears."

"It's true."

"Thanks. I feel the same about you."

I smiled, biting my bottom lip out of nerves. I looked up to see him watching me.

"I want to confess something." He moved his arm to the back of the couch and rested there as he crossed his right leg over his left. Nate was a big guy, and that was especially apparent when he sat on this monstrous couch. Nick always fell into it, but Nate very much needed the size.

"What?"

He leaned over and propped his elbows on his knees. "I started to look up Leo."

Dread filled me. He already knew the story.

"Oh."

"But Lucky came to the window, my dad came over, and I chatted with him, and then I stopped. And that's when you texted."

I nodded. "So…"

"I only found out his birthdate and his address, but I didn't bother to look it up."

"His address had been at a halfway house, but I doubt it is any longer."

Nate nodded slowly. "Ah, I see."

"I'm sure you could tell by looking at him."

"He carried himself in a certain manner. Yeah." Nate breathed out slowly. "Have you seen him recently?"

I shook my head. "No. Not for a very long time."

"I see."

My heart started pounding quicker as I looked at Nate. The kindness in his eyes defused any worries I had about telling him my past, but I was still worried that we'd never be the same. It wasn't like I got involved in anything or did anything wrong, but guilt by association and all.

I smiled at Nate and took a breath, not letting it out. "So, Leo and I were best friends since grade school."

Nate nodded. "Those kinds of friendships are special."

"They are. They can be," I corrected. The moment I started, my shoulders relaxed, and I knew I had a friend in Nate. The breath I'd been holding no longer held me captive, the worry slowly dissipating.

"We were inseparable. People in town called him our third twin." I smiled, thinking fondly of the times we'd head over to the mini-mart and pick out an ice cream bar in the summer. "He was just a really good kid put in a really lousy situation."

"Often the case," Nate said softly.

My stomach clenched, thinking about how things changed so drastically. "If someone would have asked me twenty years ago if I'd be sitting in the middle of nowhere—no offense."

He smiled. "None taken."

"And worried that Leo might track me down and do something scary to me or himself, I would have told them they were crazy." My pulse shot up, thinking about the little boy I'd loved so much. I took a sip of wine and looked outside to see a smattering of light along the lakeshore.

"Life has a shitty way of making U-turns sometimes."

I nodded in agreement. "I never thought there could have been something to rock our friendship and then inevitably destroy it."

"Drugs?"

I nodded, feeling a lump form in the back of my throat. "Yeah, lots of them."

"I'm so sorry."

"Me too." I shook my head. "This wasn't the man he was meant to be. It's just a shell of a person. I want to believe his soul is still in there, his spirit. I know it is, but…" I cleared my throat so I had something else to do other than cry. "It's hard to see through the smoke and mirrors of drugs. What's crazy is that I still love him so much."

Nate's gaze dropped to his wine glass, and he nodded.

"My sister and I had a rough childhood, and Leo did too. I think that was what bound us so tightly," I continued. "We knew that no matter how much crap went down at home, we all had one another the next day. We had each other's backs, and when you're kids, that's…"

"Everything," Nate finished.

Our eyes met, and I nodded. "So, you know."

"I do, and a loss like that is crushing."

Chapter Sixteen

Nate

Seeing the pain in Amy's eyes crushed me. She loved this man, or the boy he used to be, and seeing that kind of purity and compassion made me speechless.

It all made sense now with Millie. Amy couldn't help herself when it came to lending a hand.

She hugged her pillow tighter and let out a groan. "Life can just turn so complicated, can't it?"

"Indeed," I said softly, knowing that I understood her pain far more than she knew.

"As we grew up, it became clear that he had feelings for me," she said softly. "By high school, I realized that they were feelings I couldn't return, not like that."

Relief spread through me, and I felt awful for it. I

shouldn't have been liberated by hearing this, but I couldn't help it. I wanted Amy, and that became clear the moment she opened the door tonight.

"I tried to go along with it, but the more I did, the more he did." She scrunched her nose. "I knew it was only a matter of time before he expected the next step." She laughed. "Probably TMI."

I laughed. "Not at all. But I think I can see where this is headed."

She nodded and let out a groan of frustration. "Yes, and I could too. Even back then. So, I stayed with him through high school, and that was when I started noticing odd behavior."

My stomach knotted. I hated drugs. I hated what they did to people. The lives they destroyed. The families they broke apart.

I brought my gaze to hers and saw a little kernel of defiance. "He started hiding things from me or forgetting about plans we had. He started hanging out with the wrong group. He knew what I wanted to do, what my sister and I planned on doing once we graduated. I think on some level, that might have spurred him to get worse."

"No." I shook my head. "That's not true. Addicts will look for any reason to use. A celebratory moment or disenchantment will give them a reason to get high. The trick is that the people around them start blaming themselves for making the addict feel a certain way, making them feel like they pushed them to an event, and it's not true. Not once they're addicts."

A flicker of relief sparked through her eyes. "Thank you for saying that."

"It's the truth. Your life, your plans, didn't push him into this world. He pulled himself into it." I shook my head. "He could have followed you and your plans. He didn't."

Amy nodded and laid back against the couch cushion. "It was so horrible watching him spiral, and his parents didn't care. My parents didn't care. Nobody cared." She pushed her lips into a thin line. "So I stayed. My sister left town before me so I could be with Leo. I guess I thought I could save him or... I don't know."

"You're a good person, Amy."

"I appreciate that." She shook her head. "Because having him back in my life, even though it's on the periphery, suddenly makes me feel like a creep, like someone who just doesn't belong."

Her words were like a million stabs to my heart. "Amy, you belong here more than you know. Everyone here loves you. Even your smile brightens people's day. I see it all the time."

Her eyes stayed on mine, and I wanted to lean over and pull her close. She stretched her arms as if she were contemplating what to say next.

"The thought of you having to leave one day literally makes me nauseous," I added.

Her eyes flashed to mine. "Really?

"Yeah."

"Then why have you booked in the other direction every time you saw me?" she teased.

"Not recently," I corrected.

"No, but before…"

"Because you scared me."

Her brows raised. "How?"

"You make me *feel* again." I shook my head. "I wasn't used to that."

Confusion dotted her expression. "What do you mean? You always look like you're loving life."

I nodded. "I do, but I have done a great job at compartmentalizing. I've kind of learned to numb my emotions. Actually, I don't even think I did it consciously."

"Wow. I never would have guessed."

I nodded. "But being near you has made me experience things that I haven't for a very long time."

"Glad I could be of service," she teased, scooting a little closer.

"And that is what has scared me up until now." I shook my head. "But tonight's not about me."

Amy took a couple of sips from her wine and closed her eyes. "You're a good man, Nate."

I shook my head. "I do my best, but sometimes, that's not good enough."

Tom's email flashed into my head. I needed to look at what was inside, but I wasn't ready.

"So, you stayed behind while your sister started carving out the life you both wanted."

She nodded and let out the heaviest sigh I'd ever heard. "Yes, and I could feel my spirit get sucked into an endless void. The days turned to weeks, which turned into months and years."

"That couldn't have been easy when you saw your sister out living the life you both wanted."

"It wasn't, but I also knew that I was choosing what I understood. I was letting fear hold me back."

"What changed?"

"Leo always loved telling me how I was a goody-two-shoes, as if that were a bad thing, but it was what kept me dreaming. It finally got to the point where he wasn't even hiding his drug use, and that scared me."

"I can understand that."

"And the less I wanted to do with it or him, the more he tried to convince me to try something."

My stomach clenched at the thought.

"I never did. The last night I saw him, he'd overdosed. I was with him when it happened. He was trying to convince me to try something." She laughed sadly, shaking her head. "I don't even know what, but I refused. So, I suppose, to get back at me in his eyes, he took enough for us both, and a little more for good measure."

"Oh, Amy."

She nodded, scraping her teeth along her bottom lip as she replayed the horror of that night in her mind. "He went down instantly."

I thought back to how she handled Millie's situation and nodded slowly.

"I called the medics. They had some stuff they injected that saved him or at least got him going again until the hospital. Well, actually, it took him a long time to recover in the hospital, from what I heard. I never went to visit him."

"Narcan," I said softly, nodding. "There's a spray now."

"Yeah. Hopefully, he hasn't experienced that too, but

I don't really know that I care to find out."

"I understand that."

"Anyway, that night, everything became crystal clear. I wasn't in love with Leo, not like that. I loved him as a friend, but the fact that he was okay with trying to get me hooked on a substance terrified me. It made me realize he didn't truly understand what it meant to love somebody. I realized I couldn't save him. I couldn't protect him. But I could protect myself, and I could stop being scared to dream again."

"Wow, Amy." I shook my head, bringing my gaze back to hers.

"Yeah, so I haven't seen him since the night he overdosed in front of me, and I had hoped to keep it that way." She took another sip of wine. "But then, for some reason, my mom did the one thing I asked her not to do and gave him some of my contact information, told him what I was doing for a living…" Her eyes fastened on mine. "You probably think I'm a complete mess now."

Her words shocked me. If anything, I admired her more for her strength, tenacity, and ability to continue to show compassion. I was falling harder with every passing minute, and there wasn't a damn thing I could do about it.

"Amy, I don't know how else to put this, but…" I propped my elbow on the back cushion and turned to look at her, really look at her. "It did quite the opposite. I'm in awe of your strength, convictions, and resilience."

"Really?" She turned to be in the same position, still holding her wine glass.

"Yeah. Really, and I imagine anyone who heard your story would feel the same, but I understand wanting to keep things private."

Feeling warm from the fire, I unbuttoned my flannel shirt to expose my long-sleeve undershirt and stretched my legs.

"Thank you." She closed her eyes. "Anyway, I don't think Leo would do anything to me or anyone around me, but I just don't know and can't take that chance. So, if I can't get him out of town before Daisy and Hunter need me again, I'm going to take a hiatus. I can't bring this crap into their lives."

"What are your plans?"

She raised her glass and chuckled. "Drink more wine."

I smiled, seeing uncertainty lace through her eyes. "Amy, you really do amaze me, and you know to trust your gut."

Amy leaned her head against the back of the couch cushion. "My gut says he wants to push his way in here and steal as much stuff as he can when I'm not looking." She shook her head. "Isn't that terrible? That's the impression I have of him."

I nodded, watching her purse her lips together.

"One thing my mom managed to afford, even though our stomachs were growling, had been some kind of spendy purses, and you can probably guess that as his addiction got worse, he managed to distract me and lift a few from her closet. The next thing I knew, people around my high school were wearing them. He'd sold them for like fifty bucks."

"Yeah, I can understand your worry."

"I can't believe how much better I feel telling you these things." Her eyes met mine, and the sweetness flowing through her gaze made my heart tighten. She deserved so much better. "I've tried to bury as much about that stuff as I could, pretending I belonged in these other worlds and like I'd never seen the shady side of life."

"We all have skeletons, Amy." I nodded and let out a deep breath as tears suddenly dotted her lashes. She wiped them away and shook her head.

"Sorry."

Without thinking, I scooted closer and wrapped my arms around her. She sniffled and rested her head on my chest. Dampness spread through my shirt as tears streamed down her cheeks and she brought in a slow, quavering breath.

I pressed my lips to the top of her head, but I didn't kiss her golden-blonde hair. Instead, I let the vanilla smell I'd grown so accustomed to around Amy permeate everything about me. Her tears stopped, and I closed my eyes, feeling her hair tickling my lips.

Her body was so warm in mine and so fragile, but I knew she was full of strength, compassion, and a kindness that was rare and something I craved.

I let my breath out slowly, and she clung tighter as I attempted to scoot back. The electricity rushing between us was hard to control. I knew she felt it because her breathing quickened as I tightened my embrace.

"You deserve happiness, Amy. You deserve the world," I whispered.

She scooted back a little and lifted her chin until her eyes met mine. "Why do I feel like things might be changing between us?"

"Maybe because we both want them to," I said, watching her eyes turn a soft shade of brown as desire flicked through her gaze.

Amy's gaze didn't stray from mine as she nodded. "I think you could be onto something, Sheriff."

My thumb brushed the tip of her chin, lifting her head slightly as I leaned forward, placing a soft kiss on her mouth.

The taste of wine lingered along my lips. She closed her eyes and let out a slow breath, parting her lips as I ran my fingers along her back. I pressed my mouth to hers, feeling the warmth of her lips on mine. Her body pressed into me as our kisses turned from slow and exploring to heated and hurried, like we'd both change our minds if we didn't hurry.

I stopped, blinking my eyes open to see Amy slowly tilt her head to the side.

"I don't want to rush this, Amy. I…" I bit my lip and clenched my eyes shut, feeling the throbbing only intensify.

"I understand," she said softly.

But she didn't understand at all. I could tell by the way every single syllable hit wrongly.

My gaze flashed open, and I shook my head. "You don't understand at all, Amy. Not even a little." I caged her in as her eyes stayed locked on mine. Her gaze dipped to my mouth, and that was all it took. I leaned down to kiss her again, but this time, it didn't matter how fast we went.

I needed to feel her in my arms, her soft, sweet lips against mine.

Amy let out a little murmur as her lips parted, and I tangled my fingers through her hair, bringing her as close as humanly possible. I wanted to memorize every single thing about this moment in case she changed her mind tomorrow.

The hums of her murmurs tickled my lips as I slid my tongue into her mouth. She brought her small hands along my chest, clutching my shirt between her fingers. Without realizing it, she'd wrapped her legs around my waist, and I could feel her warmth through my jeans.

Everything about this moment made me feel like I truly knew what it was to be alive again. The scents, noises, and touches elevated me to a place I didn't even know I could reach anymore. As she sat on my lap, our kisses intensifying, my feelings turning wild, I realized that I would do anything for Amy.

It was a thought that had never occurred to me before, and that alone scared me enough to pull back as her doe eyes stared intently into mine.

Chapter Seventeen

Amy

The doorbell ringing down the hall got me out of my stupor. I stood from my bed, struggling with the sheets while my hair fell in a tangled mess over my eyes. The incessant ringing of the doorbell didn't do good things for my brain cells. I shoved the strands away with my palm so I could see better before stumbling over a pile of clothes on the floor.

My head throbbed in some sort of silent protest. I clumsily kicked the twisted sheet from my ankle and realized my world spun a little. Everything seemed to lean slightly to the right, or was it me who was leaning slightly to the side?

More ringing echoed through the house as I shuffled down the hallways, preparing myself to ward off whoever was on the other side of the door when it hit me.

Leo was in town.

Nate and I made out last night.

As I pushed my fingertips into the dull ache on the side of my head, the journey to the door felt more like an epic odyssey than a simple task of answering a door.

I made my way through the family room as the sun sprayed into the room, and I shielded my eyes from the atrocious intruder known as daylight. It was just all too much.

The dinging.

The kissing.

The drinking.

The kissing.

The dinging.

"Alright, alright." I stumbled toward the entry when I saw something that literally stopped me in my tracks.

Sprawled on the family room couch was the hulk of a sheriff, sleeping so peacefully with a pillow plopped over his head, a navy blanket stretched over his clothed, muscular body, and two feet wrapped in black wool socks. The sight brought a smile to my lips as the doorbell rang again.

As I made my way to the door, the memories from last night crashed into me with a vividness that made my stomach dip and rise like a rollercoaster—the flirtation, laughter, the conversation.

For the first time in my life, I felt heard by a man, and I didn't know what to make of it.

And the kiss, oh… the kiss that started as something flirty and playful and quickly turned into something intense and deep like a need for a special type of comfort we'd both craved.

I took a deep breath, wrapped my fingers around the handle, and flung the door open to see a deputy. He removed his cowboy hat and placed it on his chest.

"Ma'am, I hate to be a bother, but I saw the sheriff's vehicle outside, and we need his assistance with something."

My eyes widened, and I stood frozen as a hot flash of embarrassment mixed with the recognition of what it looked like happened last night.

"He's on the couch. I'll wake him up," I said, feeling my cheeks burning. "Nothing happened. He just stayed on the couch."

"None of my business either way," he said with a twinkle in his eyes.

I'd gone to so much trouble trying to avoid bringing attention to myself, and then I went and almost slept with the sheriff, one of the most well-connected men in town.

"Smooth, Amy," I muttered.

"What was that, Ma'am?"

"Oh, nothing." I grinned. "Would you like to come inside?"

He shook his head. "I'll give the sheriff some privacy."

"Okay." I shut the door and leaned against it for a brief second, taking a few breaths to clear my mind. The reality of the moment cleared my head instantly from the wine last night. There was an officer outside and the sheriff inside.

Now, I just hoped Nate wouldn't be upset about being found here. This probably wasn't great for his image. After all, he was an elected official.

I shoved myself off the door and made my way to the family room. As I came into the room, I watched him sleep for a few seconds. His chest's slow rise and fall warmed me from the outside in, and I instantly imagined what it would be like to snuggle with him on some leisurely Saturday morning.

But another part of me, the more logical and cautious part, knew that whatever this was between us worked in the moment and didn't have much of a chance to last. We both wanted different things, and our past was too divergent to come together.

Or did we want different things?

Still reeling from the intensity of last night, I cleared my throat and bent down, gently sliding my fingers along

Nate's arm.

Even if many things were blurry from last night, the kiss we shared was top of mind as well as my plan to talk to Leo and ask him to go home.

"Nate, one of your guys is here looking for you," I said softly.

He grunted a little, which made my stomach tighten with a need for something I knew I shouldn't want.

Steeling myself in a pointed direction, I lifted the pillow from his face to see him blinking his eyes open slowly and smiling at me.

"You're just as gorgeous now as last night," he said with a gruff morning voice I could get used to far too easily.

I chuckled and sat next to him. "The sunlight is blinding you. Trust me. I'm a hot mess, Nate."

A smile deepened on his lips as he shook his head. "Then I think it's safe to say you're my kind of hot mess."

His words made me giggle, and I didn't want to move a muscle. In fact, I wanted to continue from where we'd left off last night.

I stood, and Nate kicked his legs over the side of the couch. "You said one of my guys is out front?"

"Yeah. I invited him in, but he stayed put."

Nate chuckled, reaching for the flannel shirt. He

pulled it on and ran his fingers through his hair. The man was just born sexy.

"I hope you're not the talk of the town," I teased as he stood and walked over to the door.

"It could be worse." He winked at me and opened the door.

"Sorry to bother you, Sheriff." He glanced around Nate and looked at me. "But we have a bit of an issue."

"Why didn't you call in through dispatch?"

He bit his bottom lip. "It's a bit of a sensitive subject. I think you'd rather see it for yourself."

Nate glanced over his shoulder at me. "So much for a day off. I'll call you later, okay?"

I nodded as Nate slid into his boots and trudged out the door, closing it gently behind him.

One thing became obvious. I already missed the man.

Instead of making coffee, I took a quick shower, purchased a one-way Amtrak ticket, and headed out to see Abby at the coffee shop for a mocha and pastry.

After talking last night with Nate, I realized I didn't want to hide or feel captive in the house. It wasn't that I wanted confrontation, but I wanted closure.

Maybe a part of me hoped to run into Leo so I could tell him face-to-face that I needed him to leave.

By the time I reached the coffee shop, the cheeriness of the café lifted me that last little bit I needed to go before I'd made my final decision. I needed to reach out to Leo—just get it over with.

"Howdy, Amy," Abby said, grinning. "How's it going? Get a good sleep last night?"

I cocked my head slightly. "Uh, yeah. How about you?"

"Oh, my sleep was just nifty." She nodded with a wry grin. "Just swell."

Swell? My brows shot up. "Good to hear?"

"What can I get started for you?"

"I'd love a coconut mocha and an apple crumble."

"You've got it." She didn't move to the register or budge to make my drinks.

"What?"

"Oh, come on, Amy. Spill the beans, no pun intended."

"What beans?" I asked, unsure how she could possibly know a thing. It had been less than an hour.

"You know… What happened?"

"Uh, not much. I'm nursing a bit of a hangover, but—
"

She pretended to stomp her foot. "I won't make your

mocha."

"You're holding caffeine hostage unless I tell you something?" I joked. "What do you want me to tell you?"

She lit up. "Everything you feel comfortable with."

"Fine, but don't tell a soul."

"Who would I tell?" She smiled innocently as I took my card out to pay. "It's on the house today."

"Okay, so Nate came over last night." I stopped as her motions slowed. "Anyway, the next thing I knew, I was pouring Nate wine and pouring myself wine."

She spun around from the espresso machine with wide eyes. "Wait a second. Nate was at your house last night? Drinking wine?"

Oh, crap. She didn't know. If she thought last night was a big deal, she'd really flip if she found out he was there this morning, too.

"What were you talking about?" I asked, wishing I could backtrack.

"The guy sniffing around town about you. He came in here again. This time, he didn't ask me and just ordered a water and a muffin again."

"He was here again?"

She nodded. "Yeah, but Nate was at your house last night?"

"He was." I let out a heavy sigh.

"Continue." Abby gave a slight nod as she took the apple crumble out of the glass case and put it in the tiny oven behind her. I realized just what good the talk I'd had with Nate did last night. I didn't feel sheepish about my past like I thought I would. It almost felt liberating.

She handed me the mocha and cake.

"That's pretty much it."

Abby quickly reached to grab them back, but I was quicker.

"That's playing dirty." She laughed as I walked to the closest table and set my food and drink down.

I took a seat and looked around, feeling at home.

"I asked Nate to come over because of that guy."

"Is it a safety issue?" she asked.

"I don't think so, but he's someone I knew from grade school. He's lost his way in life, and I had to cut ties, but he's obviously tracked me down."

A group of customers came in, and Abby was busy making drinks as I pulled out my phone. The sky was brilliant blue, not a flake in the horizon.

The sooner I reached out to Leo, the better. I didn't need a spring snowstorm to come spiraling in and trap him in Buttercup Lake.

I waited until the customers left and moved to the table closer to the fire. Just thinking about Leo made me chilly. I could do this, and in a public place would be even better.

The sooner I spoke with him, the better it would be for my sanity. But I didn't rush. Instead, I sipped my mocha as Abby wiped down the counters before walking over.

"I'm sorry you're having to deal with this guy from your past. I once had a creepy neighbor I had to deal with." She shivered and shook her head.

"Thanks. I'm hoping to talk with him over coffee and send him on his way. I even bought him a ticket out of town."

"Well, that should send a message."

I nodded, taking a piece of crumble cake off the corner. "Yeah, and I'm still not sure it will."

"Did you want to have him come here? My husband is stopping by in a few minutes to drop off cups and lids. It might be nice to do it in a public space, and the police are never far away around here."

I smiled. "I've noticed that. You wouldn't mind?"

"Not at all."

Just as I picked up my phone, Abby's husband walked in with a cardboard box.

"Hey, sweetie," she called.

He spotted his wife, slid the box onto the table, and came over to kiss her.

"Do you mind sticking around for a little bit?"

"Not at all." He shook his head.

If this same conversation had happened yesterday, I would have been uncomfortable, but either the wine was still flowing in me somehow or the talk with Nate had helped.

"Awesome," Abby said, springing from the chair. "I'll let you be."

"Thanks, you two."

She nodded and slid her arm around his waist right before he picked up the box.

I slowly scrolled through my calls, found Leo's number, and hit the call button. My throat tightened with each unanswered ring until he finally picked up.

Chapter Eighteen

Nate

I looked down at the shattered glass on the floor and sighed deeply as the drapes blew from the wind.

"We thought you'd want to know right away." The officer glanced at me. "I just didn't expect it to be a mule."

I nodded, twisting my lips into a contemplative whistle as I stared at Lucky inside the dining room. She'd managed to burst through the single French door on the side of my porch that led into the dining room. It was the only door in my house besides the slider that had a glass entry. The glass pane had shattered, and true to Lucky's name, she'd made it inside unscathed.

And that was where she'd stayed while my deputies tracked me down.

Now, she just stared at me.

Well, we stared at each other. The ridiculousness of the circumstances rendered me perplexed. Had she not snuck back to my home more than once, I would have thought nothing of it. Farm animals go rogue from time to time, but this was something more.

"Hey, Son. I saw the ruckus and noticed she was missing." My dad came up behind me and slapped my shoulder. "She's really got a thing for you."

"It's odd." I turned to look at my dad and folded my arms over my chest. "Don't you think?"

"I do, actually." He nodded.

I walked through the opening, and the mule's ears twitched. She looked at me with her big, brown eyes and didn't move, but she let out a soft bray to greet me.

My dad followed behind me while the mule seemed unaware of the havoc it had just caused in my dining room. I'd gone through a lot of hostage negotiation training before to get people outside, but it never included rogue equines.

"Come on, Lucky. Let's see what you're really thinking." I took a step closer and reached out to scratch behind her ear. With some gentle coaxing, I should be able to lead her through the kitchen and out the back.

"You know she's just going to keep on coming back,

don't you?" my dad asked.

"It does appear that way."

"Spring's coming. I bet we could get a quick shed up for her to stay in during rough weather."
My dad stood next to me. "You've got a pen out there she can roam in."

"You're giving up on Lucky?" I asked, surprised.

"No, but I don't tend to fight the obvious." My dad handed me the lead, and I fastened it around her as she clopped through my house and out onto my patio.

"I don't know. I just think there's something fishy about Lucky's infatuation."

My dad laughed, following me outside. "I can't imagine what that would be."

I shook my head, realizing how crazy I sounded.

But my gut said there was something to it. In addition to looking at Tom's email tonight, I'd also make sure to look up why a mule might get this way.

"Hey, you want the name of my brother's glass shop?" one of the deputies asked. He poked his head outside and looked over at me. "He has a shop about fifteen minutes away. He's the guy who fixed Grace's place when the white deer broke inside."

"That'd be great. Thanks." I nodded, sliding out my

phone.

"Sure thing. I'll give him a shout and text you his information."

"Thanks." I gave a quick nod and ran my hand along Lucky's neck. She felt like she needed someone, and I didn't want to keep giving her back.

"Well, I'd better fasten a board up and get Lucky to her new home."

"So, you're keeping her?"

I nodded. "For the time being."

My dad smiled with approval as my phone buzzed.

Did you know that Amy is meeting with that guy? She's at my coffee shop now waiting for him.

I froze in place and glanced at my dad. "I'm sorry to ask this, but can you take care of Lucky? Get her situated over there?" I pointed at the fenced area on my property. It was about an acre of pasture. If she were going to stay longer, I might enlarge the area since I didn't have much back there.

"Sure." My dad took over the lead. "Everything okay?"

"Yeah. I think so. Thanks, Dad."

I marched through the field toward my house when

the officer with the brother came outside. "He's doing a job about five minutes away and will come over next."

"You've just scored major points," I said, nodding. "Thanks. I really appreciate it. I have to take off, but keep me posted."

"I'll stay here until he gets here since it's open."

The other squad cars had left the property since Lucky was the culprit and there wasn't some villainous crime spree taking place.

"I really appreciate it. Coffee is on me tomorrow," I told him.

He tipped his hat as I hurried to my SUV and climbed in.

What was she thinking, meeting him? At least she chose a public location. Last night, we'd bounced around the idea of talking to Leo and getting things out in the open, maybe even buying a bus ticket out of town, but I didn't expect her to track him down and execute the plan in less than twenty-four hours.

I laughed at the thought as my grip tightened on the wheel. She'd certainly keep me busy. The woman didn't let any grass grow under her feet, and I'd be lying if I didn't admit that was a complete turn-on.

Who was I kidding? Everything about Amy turned

me on. I was a living, breathing horn ball around her. This morning, I almost wrapped my arms around her and brought her down on top of me. What stopped me was that I wanted to brush my teeth, and an officer was waiting outside her door.

But just the thought of her possibly being in harm's way made me step on the gas a little harder.

By the time I'd gotten to town and parked out front, I'd worked myself into the worried boyfriend that I wasn't.

Not yet, anyway.

I made my way inside and immediately spotted Amy by the fireplace talking to someone, who was clearly a male from seeing the back of him. Judging by his build, hair color, and clothes, it was Leo. Abby eyed me, and her husband gave a quick wave.

Amy didn't seem to notice that I'd come in, which worried me. Deep conversation with an addict could go really sideways, and last night, she'd seemed so much freer before she'd fallen asleep. It felt like progress had been made, and now, I didn't know what to think.

"Your usual?"

I gave a quick nod. "Sounds good."

"They've been talking for about twenty minutes."

"Anything sound… aggressive?"

Abby shook her head. "No, but Amy hasn't so much

as looked in our direction or taken a sip from her mocha."

I didn't want to intrude, but I felt an overwhelming desire to protect Amy, both physically and mentally. I'd failed to do this once already in my life, and it had cost me almost everything. I refused to let that happen again.

To most people, it might look like a pleasant exchange of two friends or something more, but I knew better. The tension she carried propped her shoulders a little higher than usual, and the constant motion of her fingertips drawing circles onto the table told me she wasn't comfortable. She leaned into her other hand as it pressed into her neck while watching Leo.

She wouldn't take her eyes off him as if she were worried that he'd steal something from her if she looked away. And maybe she was right, but it might not be physical.

I leaned against the counter as Abby handed me the drink. I was just out of Abby's view, but I could see Leo clearly.

Nerves twisted uncomfortably inside me as I looked on, watching Leo's manipulative ways coat his every word. I could see it with every flick of his gaze, the motion of his hands, the slow movement toward her before sliding back in his chair. Seeing them together stirred a deep protectiveness within me.

I wasn't jealous.

Or maybe I was.

I didn't want to be.

But I was here mainly to ensure Amy and everyone else's safety. Domestic disputes could become some of the worst in an instant.

I heard forced laughter from Amy. A sound I'd never heard before, and my spine tingled. She felt obligated to keep him happy, and that discomfort concerned me.

Leo sat back in his chair with a clunk. He sulked, crossing his arms over his chest.

Oh, no. Things could get salty really quickly. I put my drink down and watched intently, straining to hear.

But Leo went into a sudden fit, standing and knocking over his chair. "You think you can just buy my way out of here?"

Oh, no. She'd offered him money or bought him a ticket.

She really did work fast.

I glanced at Abby and her husband. He looked like he was ready to join me with whatever might go down, which I hoped was absolutely nothing.

Amy's voice rose as she pleaded with Leo to calm down. He looked like a child who hadn't gotten his way.

Tipping his chair upright from the ground, he sat in it with a thud.

My palms grew clammy, not because I was worried about how this would end, but because I could feel the tension rolling off Amy. The one thing she didn't want in town was a scene, and Leo was ensuring that he created one.

But I knew Abby and her husband wouldn't say a word. This secret would be safe inside these walls. No customers had come in or out since I'd arrived.

"You never loved me, Amy." Leo's words hung in the air.

I didn't hear any response. Only silence filled the air. I wanted to rush in and pull Amy from the wreck Leo had become, save her from the harsh words that were meant to scar, not heal.

But to my surprise, Amy didn't need rescuing.

She cleared her throat, pushed back the chair, and let out a laugh. "Leo, I loved you as a friend from the moment we played at recess together, but I love myself more. I have nothing for you. I won't open my life up to you. That night, you almost died, but you wanted to take me with you, and I will never forget that. I've forgiven you, but I haven't forgotten. Take this ticket and go home. Get help."

The stillness in the coffee shop created a fire of

tension. Her voice had been loud enough for us all to hear. She didn't care. Her skeletons were no longer pulling her into a quiet grave.

I stepped out from where I'd been standing with my drink, and Amy's gaze instantly connected with mine.

As I'd suspected, she was standing, towering over the man she'd once cared for more deeply than herself. She'd said her piece.

Amy straightened and drew a breath. "I'm sure the sheriff can give you a ride to the bus depot."

I took a few steps forward. "Absolutely."

Leo jerked up, nearly toppling Amy's drink. "No, I can find my way there."

Amy's eyes pleaded with me, and I gave a quick nod. "We don't have a great taxi service here. Why don't you let me do the honor?"

Leo spun around, surprised to hear me. He recognized my uniform, not me.

"I ain't high, man," he said, scowling at me.

"Never said you were, but I did hear that Miss Nichols went to the trouble to buy you a ticket home."

He scratched his scalp and twitched, glancing around the coffee shop. "I don't have any money for food on the way."

An addict's life was built upon excuses.

Abby came from behind the counter with a small paper bag. "I've filled it with some bottled water, a couple of cans of sodas, croissants, French rolls, and brownies. I threw in some bags of nuts, too."

Uncertainty darted through his gaze as he looked at Abby and then over at Amy. He reached for the bag from Abby and stood motionless.

"I ain't never had people go to so much effort to get me out of town," he said sarcastically.

Abby went back to where her husband stood. He wrapped his arm around her before going to the back room where they kept the supplies.

"It's not that, Leo," Amy said softly. "But I know why you're here, and I won't let you steal from the people who care for me, who've welcomed me into their home with open arms."

His gaze flicked to me and then back to Amy. "I wasn't going to steal nothin'. I just wanted a place to crash."

"It's not my home to offer, and I don't know you, Leo. I don't know the man you've become. I only know the boy I once loved, and I no longer see him."

Leo started to say something. His jaw twitched, his mouth opened, but he shut it quickly. Instead, he turned and faced me.

"Ready?"

He nodded without giving Amy another look. "Yeah."

"Goodbye, Leo. I wish you nothing but the strength you need to get better."

Leo walked in front of me and pushed open the door. I glanced over my shoulder to see Amy sink into the chair, and I wanted nothing more than to run back inside to comfort her, but I knew making sure Leo got on the bus would be the biggest gift I could give her, and that was what I intended to do.

Chapter Nineteen

Amy

As soon as Nate led Leo away, I wanted to crumple into a pile of tears. Not because I was sad that he was leaving or that I couldn't get through to him.

But because I didn't know I could be that strong. They were tears of surprise.

And I realized he didn't want help.

He wanted things from me, things that didn't belong to him, so he could continue doing the only thing he knew how to do.

Get high.

For whatever reason, his old stomping ground had lost its appeal, but I hoped he felt that a person was seen in Buttercup Lake.

He would be seen.

He would be watched.

He would be uncomfortable.

His life wouldn't be easy, his actions wouldn't be ignored, and jail wouldn't be far away.

For a brief spell, it felt selfish to want that, for him to go away. But sometimes, to save one life rather than destroy two, you had to make a choice, and I chose me.

When I watched Nate's SUV drive away, I profusely apologized to Abby and her husband for bringing that drama to their little slice of heaven, but they told me there wasn't anything to apologize for and hugged me until the tension left my body.

She also quickly reminded me of the Sunshine Breakfast Club's meeting tonight.

When I said my goodbyes, I knew that my secret was safe with them. They understood it was my story to tell if I ever wanted to speak of it, and if I didn't, that was my right as well.

But now that I sat in the quiet of Nick and Brielle's home, I felt eerily at peace. I didn't know if I'd be staying in Buttercup Lake forever, but the idea of it didn't seem so scary.

Going to the book club tonight seemed like a good idea—something lighter to ground me in this reality I chose.

When I looked into Leo's eyes today, I realized it wasn't the small town's fault. I realized fault didn't even matter. Finding someone or something to blame wouldn't change the outcome. It wouldn't make anyone feel better. It wouldn't make Leo stop using. It would only give a false sense of security because the truth was that what happened to Leo could happen to anyone, anywhere.

The thing about Buttercup Lake was that it represented a place so far removed from it all that I could imagine a life where these things didn't exist. I could watch little Tate, sleep on my expensive sheets, and pretend that my past wasn't part of me.

But that didn't make me whole.

And talking with Nate last night about things made that abundantly clear. My past made me who I was in this very second. It was okay to want to be complete, to feel grounded in the choices I'd made to get me here, away from a life that wasn't satisfying.

I wiped away a stray tear when my doorbell rang. Scooting the blanket off my lap, I stood up and walked over to answer it.

"Who is it?"

"Nate," he said through the door.

My stomach did a little somersault at the news, and I

flung open the door.

"You're not in uniform?"

His brows raised, and he pointed over his shoulder. "Did you want me to go put it on?"

I chuckled, reached for his shirt, fisted the fabric between my fingers, and pulled him in.

Placing his mouth on mine, he gently kicked the door closed behind him and pulled me closer, wrapping his arms around my waist. The softness of his lips against mine made my body fall into him, letting me forget about the day.

My eyes closed, and he picked me up and carried me to the couch. His kisses still ignited everything inside me like a new beginning. He softly nipped my bottom lip as I moaned a little, and my hands ran under his shirt.

My fingertips felt the hardness of his abs all the way to the indents of his pecs, and I couldn't help but smile as he kissed me harder. His hands fluttered under my shirt as his fingers skimmed my belly, creating a frenzy of desire in me as the pillows caught me and he knelt over me.

I opened my eyes to see his beautiful hazel eyes taking me in.

"What?" I asked, breathless, as he tilted his head slightly.

"You're just the strongest woman I know."

I pretended to flex my arm muscle, and he shook his head. "You know what I mean."

"I didn't know what I was going to do when he showed up at the coffee shop. When I texted him, I think I was going off adrenaline from the night before... you know, when we made out."

Nate chuckled.

"But once he got there, I just felt so many emotions running through me. I was mad, sad, hurt, frustrated, you name it, but then I realized that he didn't have that control over me unless I let him." I kept my eyes on Nate. "But I believe my clarity is thanks to you."

I scooted up, and he sat back. "How so?"

"I've been so busy pointing my finger at the town I grew up in that I never gave myself credit." I grinned. "And all it takes is one look at you to see how amazing small towns can be."

"I often have that effect on people," he added, winking.

I pretended to smack him and shook my head. "I'm serious. I just feel so much... freer."

He pulled my hands into his and smiled. "I know exactly what you mean."

"You do?"

Nate nodded, letting go of my hands.

"Wait. What time is it?" I asked.

"A few minutes before five. Why?"

"Oh, no. I must have been staring at the wall for too long." I shot up. "I'm going to be late for the book club meeting tonight, and I promised Abby I'd be there."

"We'll get there in time. Grab your book and coat and meet me out front."

I nodded, feeling a self-imposed wave of urgency, but after what I'd just put Abby through, I had to stand by my word.

Nate went outside, and I grabbed a bag of potato chips, the dip out of the fridge, and my book.

By the time I got to his vehicle, he had the heater blasting and music playing.

"You ready?"

I looked at him. "You're not going to flip the siren on, are you?"

He chuckled. "No."

"Thank goodness." I smiled, buckling up as he pulled out of the driveway.

We drove onto the road, and I saw Daisy and Hunter putting Tate into his car seat across the street. Daisy waved at me, and Nate slowed, rolling my window down.

"Going to the book club?" Daisy asked.

"Sure am. You?"

She nodded. "Hunter is taking Tate grocery shopping."

"Would he like company?" Nate joked.

Daisy laughed. "He probably would. Okay. See ya there."

Nate rolled up the window, and on our way we went.

"That seemed normal," I said, glancing at Nate.

"Why wouldn't it? You worried about the Leo thing?"

I shook my head. "No, I meant us driving together."

Nate smiled and nodded.

"Are you worried about what people will say?" I asked.

"What, precisely, do you think might get them gossiping?" he asked, glancing at me. I caught a smirk dash across his features as I thought about it.

"You're right. We've only kissed."

"Just to set the record straight, though, I've never experienced a kiss like that." His smile widened as he turned the corner and looked at me.

"Which part? Duration? Sparks?" I joked.

"All of the above."

I snuck a look at him. "Same."

A few minutes of comfortable silence stirred between us.

"Just so you feel better about things, I want you to know that I waited until the bus drove away before I left the station."

Surprisingly, it did make me feel better. I felt the last little bit of tension I'd been hanging on to drift away.

"Thanks for doing that. It actually does. He would definitely be the type who'd pretend to get on and jump out the moment he thought he could."

He nodded. "I thought it might make you feel better."

There was one question I'd wanted to ask, but I wasn't sure how it would come across.

"Did he say anything on the ride over?"

Nate shifted slightly in his seat, and he nodded. "He did, but not much."

When he didn't offer up what was exchanged, I took it as a sign to let it go. It didn't matter, anyway.

The community center came into view, and Nate slowed.

"You're sure you're ready for this?"

Nate's low rumble of a laugh drifted through the vehicle, and I couldn't help but smile.

"Let 'em talk." He winked at me, and I unbuckled.

"If you say so."

"Back in an hour?"

I nodded and climbed out of the SUV, carefully balancing the chips, dip, and my book as I shut the door with my hip. It didn't close all the way, so Nate leaned over and somehow managed to open and shut it with one fell swoop.

As Nate pulled away, Hunter pulled up with Daisy waving through the window.

She turned around in her seat, gave Tate a little tug on his leg, and blew a kiss to him before climbing out. I wanted to go say hi to him, but I knew that might start an entire baby meltdown.

Daisy climbed out of their car with a bowl of something green. I narrowed my eyes.

"Broccoli salad?" I asked, recognizing the bacon bits.

"Yup." Daisy nodded, smiling. "So, how did I do?"

I looked at her, perplexed, as we started to walk to the entrance. "With what?"

"You know… playing it cool with Nate driving you here."

I chuckled and shook my head as Daisy opened the door.

"I don't know what you're talking about."

Daisy laughed as she let the door shut behind us.

"And you're doing a terrible job of playing like nothing is going on between you two."

I rolled my eyes and shook my head just as I heard Millie's laughter roll through the halls.

"She's here?"

Daisy shrugged. "Certainly sounds like it unless they figured a way to pipe in a recording."

As we walked by the leprechaun disguised as a giving tree, or vice-versa, I slowed.

"Would you mind pulling one of those off? I keep forgetting, and St. Paddy's Day is almost here."

"Sure." She stopped and looked at me. "Does it matter which one?"

I shrugged. "How about the one at the top?"

"Sounds good." She pulled the tag off and stuffed the small green paper into my purse for me.

When we got to the right room, I immediately spotted the buffet table and several familiar faces, but I didn't see Millie. I was certain I heard her laugh, though.

We made our way to the buffet table and set everything down when I heard Millie again.

I spun around to see Grace and Nina and realized Millie was on Zoom. Filling up my plate with broccoli salad, tea sandwiches, salami, and tater tot casserole, I made my way to the sisters.

"Hey, Amy," Grace gushed. "I'm so glad you made it."

I chuckled, sitting next to Nina while I balanced the plate on my knees.

"Wouldn't miss it for the world," I said dryly. How I'd managed to fit a few chapters with everything in my world going sideways, I didn't know. But it was a great escape, and the sheriff in the book was lovable and so protective.

Millie eyed me from the screen. "What kind of food you got there?"

"A little of everything, but it's only round one. I plan on binging on some cheesy bread and veggies and dip on my next round."

"Good girl. I wish I could be there, but Grace and Nina are taking the doctor's orders quite literally," she grumped.

I chuckled. "Probably a good idea they're doing that, Millie."

She scowled. "You sound just like them."

"Because we love you," Grace chided.

Millie rolled her eyes and took a sip of V8 juice.

"That looks good," I offered.

"I've had better. I'd like some of what you've got on

your plate, but my great-granddaughter and Jackson Sr. took away all my snacks. I can either have fruit or vegetables. That's it. I didn't get this old just eating fiber and seeds. And did you even know they made low-sodium V8? Why? I'm even stuck with that too."

I laughed, trading glances with Grace. Millie left off right where she'd been before the stroke.

"Your doctor probably wants you to have a low-sodium diet," I said gently.

"What's next? No sugar?" She took a sip from her can of tomato juice.

I felt bad for eating in front of her, so I waited until Grace turned the screen away.

Abby waltzed into the room with a platter full of pastries from the coffee shop, and I waved.

Her eyes connected with mine, and she flashed a warm smile in my direction.

So far, so good.

She grabbed a plate and started piling it high before taking a seat across from us.

"Okay, let's get to business." Millie coughed, and Grace turned the screen around so everyone could see Millie's face propped on the seat. "Amy, did you enjoy kissing the sheriff?"

My gaze snapped to Abby's, and she grinned.

She might not tell a soul about Leo, but apparently, Nate and I were fair game. Just thinking about Nate made me miss him.

I was definitely falling for the man with the badge. I chuckled to myself and realized that maybe for the first time ever, my picker was alright.

Chapter Twenty

Nate

Lucky hadn't tried to escape once since being at my house. I wasn't sure what it meant, but I knew it was some sort of sign.

For what?

I had no idea.

It had been a few days since I last saw Amy after taking her home from the book club. I wasn't feeling as ornery about the members anymore, either.

But I was still extremely suspicious.

It was Saturday morning, and tomorrow was St. Paddy's Day. I usually didn't do a thing for it except, once in a blue moon, share a Guinness with my Dad.

But for some reason, I wanted to get out, celebrate,

231

and bring along my favorite person.

I knew the restaurant downtown next to the coffee shop was doing a themed menu tomorrow night. It might be fun to hang out with Amy, and it would give me an excuse to see her again.

She'd been through a lot in recent weeks, so I didn't want to come on too strongly. But a part of me figured it was too late for that. The only thing that kept me from kissing her was to stay away. And the only reason I'd done that the last few days was because I'd been swamped at work, and she'd been looking after Tate.

I also hadn't looked at my email from Tom. It wasn't that I didn't think it was important. I did, but I'd been so preoccupied with work and Amy that I'd put it in the back of my mind, and I shouldn't have.

Just because he hadn't spoken to me in over a decade didn't make me mad at him. In fact, my feelings toward Tom and his family were quite contrary to that. I missed them.

But I understood.

I sat on my couch and stared out the window to see Lucky trotting in her pasture. She seemed so free and happy.

Dare I say content?

She hadn't tried slipping out since we'd let her be here.

I opened my laptop, moved my cursor to my inbox, and hovered over Tom's name. It wasn't like I was scared.

Or was it?

There wasn't a damn thing I could do to change the past, but I owed it to them and myself to see what Tom wanted. I was pretty certain it wasn't friendship.

That would be asking too much, under the circumstances. I thought back to Amy and Leo, the friendship from a young age that bound them together through many life obstacles. Except one flourished, and the other withered until the relationship was no more.

The problem was that when I thought about Tom and me, I wasn't sure which was which, and I worried neither of us had flourished.

I'd spent the last decade running from connections, and that became even more apparent once Amy bounded into my life, and I hoped with all my heart that didn't happen to Tom.

However, he was reaching out for a reason, and I had to respect that. I needed to read his message. After all, I owed it to him, his family, and most of all, Ella.

I clenched my teeth and ground my molars together, thinking back to that fateful night. How our entire lives had changed from one simple act after a chain of events that I never could have predicted.

Letting out a heavy sigh, I clicked on the message, which appeared in full view just as the doorbell rang.

I instinctively glanced back to ensure Lucky was where she needed to be and smiled. It wasn't her ringing the bell.

Moving the laptop aside, I stood and walked over to the door, opening it to see Amy smiling, all bundled up with a purple knit cap pulled over her ears, holding a pie.

"Surprise. I thought we could use something sweet."

Man, she was adorable. I took the pie from her gloved hands and welcomed her inside.

I slid a kiss along her cheek and caught her closing her eyes.

"This smells incredible."

"It's my specialty," she said, grinning as she unbuttoned her coat.

I loved the thought of Amy making herself comfortable. She hung her coat in the closet in the entryway as I watched her move through my house like she belonged here.

"I only got to see the foyer last time, but your house is…" Amy pressed her lips together and brought her gaze to mine.

What was she going to say?

Messy?

Cluttered?

Or the opposite?

Too clean?

Too sterile?

"Absolutely perfect," she said softly. "And that porch out front. I don't think I've ever told you, but I've always loved porches. They always seemed so welcoming."

I smiled at Amy as I held the pie, watching her appear like a whirlwind dashing from the closet to the wall of family photographs.

"You mentioned you loved old farmhouses and one-room cabins, but I don't think you said anything about a porch."

She spun around, eyeing me. "Good memory. Your brother looks so much like you."

I laughed. "Don't let him hear you say that."

She chuckled. "Ah, one of those relationships."

"He's very much his own man."

"What does he do?"

"He's a cop in another state."

"Big city?" she teased.

"Something like that. He's married."

Her eyes fastened on mine, and I felt that familiar charge pulse through me. "Really."

I nodded.

"Is that something you want to do someday?" she asked.

Two months ago? No. Today? I wasn't so sure.

"I'm not totally against it."

She laughed, tipping her chin. "That's the spirit."

"What about you?"

"Oh, yeah. I want the whole thing. Huge wedding. Husband. Amazing honeymoon. A dog. Kids. A house to stick them all in. Yeah. I've wanted it as long as I could remember."

Her revelation surprised me. That was a long time to hold on to a dream.

I glanced down at the pie, smelling the sweetness as it drifted through the air. "Would you like a slice?"

"I'd love one." She followed me into the kitchen at a slower pace. I noticed her hanging back, looking at my few knickknacks and photos on a shelf.

She reached for a small photo, and my stomach clenched. "Is this another brother I don't know about?"

I shook my head, setting the pie on the counter. "No. It's… He's an old friend."

"Does he live in Buttercup Lake? He's kind of cute."

I laughed and looked over at Amy as she flashed a wry grin.

"No, we actually haven't spoken in over a decade, a little longer."

She set the photo back down and studied me quietly, probably expecting to say something more.

Instead, I reached for some plates and a knife and started cutting into the pie.

Amy slowly walked into the kitchen and spotted the coffee pot. "Would you like some coffee to go with the pie? I can make some while you serve us up."

"Sounds wonderful." I nodded, relieved she didn't pry about Tom.

The guilt started weighing heavily, considering I still hadn't read his message.

I stepped aside to let her reach the coffee grounds in a canister I had next to the coffee pot. She quietly scooped them into the filter and poured water into the machine.

Her unexpected presence in my home warmed me in a way I hadn't expected. Besides a few buddies, coworkers, and my family, I hadn't had that many people in my space.

Especially not women.

I just never had time.

It was never a priority.

I watched Amy move through my kitchen with careful ease, reaching for some napkins and opening some drawers until she found the one with the utensils.

"You're so tidy," she said, laughing. "Everything has its place."

"You didn't expect it?"

She shook her head and shrugged. "I'm not sure what I expected, but it's a nice surprise."

"You deserve one once in a while."

Amy laughed, and the melody traveled through the kitchen, warming the space even more. "It has definitely been an interesting few weeks." She reached for the plate with the smaller slice on it. "But they've been informative, and some good things have come out of them."

"Yeah?" I teased. "Like what?"

"Oh, I don't know." She stood with the plate in her hands. "Seeing what it's like to fall for a good guy, for once."

I wasn't sure which part of that statement to unpack first, so I went with the easiest.

"You're falling for me, Amy? Is that what you're saying?"

She put the fork into her mouth, a little bit of cherry stuck to her lip. "Isn't it obvious? You know, bringing you cherry pie when it's twenty degrees outside."

I laughed. "Tomorrow, it's supposed to be in the forties. You could have waited."

She playfully batted her napkin at me and shook her head. "Spring is finally here."

I took a bite of the cherry pie, the flavors bursting in my mouth. When I'd finished chewing, I shook my head. "Wow, Amy. This is incredible."

"You like it?"

"You can make this for me anytime."

"And lose your six-pack? I don't think so."

I chuckled, shaking my head. "I suddenly feel objectified. And who said I have one? You haven't seen me without my shirt."

She grinned, forking in another bite. "My fingers wouldn't lie to me. I felt those muscles when we kissed." She winked at me, and I laughed.

There was something about being with Amy that just made things in my life feel good.

That was a feeling I hadn't really let myself feel for a long time.

"Want to sit on the couch?"

"I'd love to," she said, following me into the great room.

The sun hadn't gone down yet, and Lucky was still

roaming the fenced-in pasture.

She followed my gaze outside as she sat down on the couch. "Wait a second. Is that the mule?"

"In all her glorious beauty."

"I thought your parents were watching her."

"They were, but she kept escaping. In fact, before everything happened with Leo, I was going to stop by and tell you about how Lucky broke into my house, shattered the glass... made a mess."

Her brows raised as a fit of laughter erupted from her belly. "She has a crush on you."

"Amy, she's a mule."

She smiled wider and took another bite, and I did the same. "I'm telling you, for whatever reason, Lucky is infatuated with you. She's imprinted on you."

I scowled and laughed harder. "Sorry, but I don't believe in that sparkly vampire stuff."

Her expression fell, and I wondered if I just broke her heart. "How do you know about sparkly vampires?"

"Seriously? I lived through a decade of the books and movies."

And then I realized why...

Because of Ella.

Tom's sister loved everything about *Twilight*, which

meant we had to take her to all the movies, sit with her in front of a bookstore before the release… the whole shebang.

"Are you okay? I didn't mean to offend you."

My gaze flashed to Amy's, and I shook my head. "No. Not at all. Sorry. I just spaced out a little."

"Yeah, I figured." She slid her hand to my knee. "You know you can tell me anything, right? I know I've used that privilege. I'd like you to, as well." Her eyes stayed on mine, but there was something different in her gaze, maybe a silent pleading.

I let out a deep breath and smiled. "I know, and I thank you for that." I took another bite of pie and let out a happy little grunt. "And this pie is incredible."

"I think you're pretty incredible," she said softly, putting her plate on the coffee table and moving closer to me.

Amy's eyes fastened on mine, and she took my plate away, putting it next to hers as she crawled on my lap.

Her dark golden, almost brown, hair splayed along my shoulders as she hung her head closer, tipping her chin down, dipping her gaze to mine.

She dropped her mouth to my ear. "It's getting harder and harder to resist you, Sheriff."

I gently held her chin and tipped my mouth to hers. We were eye to eye, searching for the next hit from each other.

Her warm breath and the sweet smells of cherry and vanilla brushed over me as my eyes stayed steady on hers, my fingers combing through her hair. The sensations sweeping through me were nearly unbearable—the aches so strong that they teetered on painful.

Amy licked her lips as her breathing quickened, and I lost all restraint, pulling her head down, her mouth colliding with mine.

The kisses skipped over the soft, gentle sweep of our tongues, trading for something raw and harder, more demanding. The hunger between us only grew as I cupped her butt and spun around on the couch.

Our kisses never broke as her hands ran under my shirt, skating over my warm skin.

I knew I'd found my slice of heaven, but I didn't know if I could be hers. She pulled back, and I knew I'd just have to go back to daydreaming about sleeping with Amy.

Chapter Twenty-One

Amy

"You weren't kidding, Amy," Abby said, taking another bite of pie. "This is hands down the best cherry pie I've ever eaten."

"Thanks. It's the bit of almond extract," I revealed. "And a little whisky."

"You put whisky in this? I had no idea."

I nodded, still buzzing from last night. Nate and I hadn't taken that next step. It almost happened, but I pulled away.

I didn't even know why because every single cell in my body was on fire for him. Things had pulsed and ached that I didn't even know could be bothered to notice.

243

Daisy nodded. "Yeah, I'm so glad she nannies for Tate because Amy's baking skills are out of this world."

"Aw, shucks." I chuckled.

Abby took another bite. "How are things going with Nate?"

The question took me by surprise. I didn't really think there was much to tell. I was falling hard for him, but we were just kind of stuck in that murky zone of... questioning. Wanting? Confusion?

I nodded. "Good."

Daisy shook her head. "I know that tone. Good... but?"

I groaned, slouched into the chair a little, and took a sip of unsweetened iced tea. "You guys. I don't kiss and tell."

"To *tell* would mean a kiss happened... again?" Abby's brow arched as she eyed me optimistically.

"Fine. Yes. We keep kissing. A lot." I laughed. "And I like it. I'm pretty sure he likes it too, but it's complicated."

I glanced at Abby, knowing she understood what I meant by that with Leo and just... life. But I felt bad for not including Daisy since she'd been my first real friend out here. I knew I'd have to tell her sooner or later.

"Nothing with the sheriff can be too complicated," Daisy teased. "He's pretty blunt. Honestly, the fact that you've even gotten him to kiss you is incredible. I kind of thought he'd just be one of those loners drifting through life until the end."

I flinched. "That's kind of bleak."

"Well, maybe he's not *that* bad, but he just never seemed to connect with anyone," Daisy said.

That was when it hit me. I wasn't sure he'd connected with me, either. Sure, our chemistry was on fire, but was that enough? I'd managed to bare my soul, yet I could feel the secrets he'd kept from me only burying themselves deeper.

I'd get little glimpses.

He had a best friend like I did.

His friendship had been since childhood.

Then I'd hear nothing again.

And then another little tidbit about loss would creep into our conversation.

And then nothing.

Any real opening to me was closed off, and I was falling harder and harder for him each passing week.

But I knew I couldn't do that to myself again, wind up with a man who couldn't open his heart fully to me.

I think that's what stopped me last night—the heaviness in my heart when I thought about all the unexplored emotions in his own.

And worse, my inability to unlock them. The space between my growing love and his started to fill with deafening silence.

I knew there was no way to really continue with him if his burdens were only his own. If he left me to wonder what inner turmoil churned inside him, it wasn't fair to me or to him.

We needed to go deeper. He saw my mess, and I wanted to see his. Maybe it wasn't messy at all. I wouldn't know because he didn't let me in.

When I went to his house last night and wandered his halls, picked up photos, and touched his knickknacks, that was when it occurred to me that he'd built a fortress around his heart, one of stoic solitude that could be seen as admirable to outsiders.

But that was precisely the problem.

I didn't want to be an outsider. My heart told me he was my person, but my head knew it took more than that. I needed the trust to run both ways, or the communication would be stunted. I couldn't pour out my heart and soul into a silent rebuttal.

I couldn't help but wonder if maybe I just wasn't enough for him, and in his heart, he knew it and didn't want to risk that next step.

Opening up.

I'd hoped not, but I couldn't understand the secrets, and I could see him slowly retreating into himself, letting the silence stretch and build the walls around his heart.

That worried me. A lot.

I worried for the day when the smile wouldn't reach his eyes any longer because he'd kept his soul from opening up, and instead, his spirit just... withered to a quiet nothing. That moment when you just existed. There were no highs and lows. Just indifference.

The thought scared me to death... enough to stop making out with him last night, even though every part of my body screamed for more.

"And then we wanted to thank you for taking such good care of our little Tate," Daisy said. She'd obviously been talking for quite some time.

I snapped to and nodded.

"Did you hear a thing I said?" she teased.

My cheeks blushed. "Sorry. Just kind of spaced."

"Oh, no. You've been spending too much time around Nate." Abby groaned.

My gaze moved to hers. "You've noticed he does that?"

"Oh, yeah. That's a Nate trait."

"I see." I laughed nervously. "I was starting to take it personally."

Abby laughed and shook her head. "Nah. Don't do that."

Daisy reached into her bag as Tate reached for a piece of banana muffin, which tumbled to the floor. He let out a wail. Abby dashed to the counter, grabbed another one, and I quickly cleaned up the mess.

Within an instant, Daisy bounced Tate on her lap while Abby handed them a new banana muffin.

"Third time's a charm." Daisy chuckled, pushing an envelope toward me with my name on it.

Was this my layoff notice? I looked at Daisy cautiously.

"Go on. Open it."

I took the envelope and slid my finger under the flap.

"It's a little way of saying thank you from us." She grinned as I looked down at a beautiful floral note. I flipped it open to see a gift card.

"It's to the Honey Leaf Lodge across the way," Daisy explained. "It's really cool."

"Oh, my word. My sister told me about their petting zoo."

Daisy nodded. "Yup. That's the place. Hunter and I

thought you could use a night away."

"Wow." I held the card up to my chest. "You have no idea how much this means."

"Well, you do so much for us, Amy. It's just like stopping by the store this morning to get groceries. I felt guilty for asking, but Tate threw up all over the couch cushions, and my morning just went sideways after that. The thought of having to get groceries just made me... sad."

I chuckled. "It's a lot being a mama. Besides, I had to pick up everything from the giving tree, Leprechaun, or whatever. I dropped it off this morning."

Daisy continued bouncing Tate on her knee and looked at me. "Have you ever thought about having kids?"

I wanted to yell at the top of my lungs, *all the time.* But I just smiled and nodded. "I do. I hope I'm lucky enough to experience being a mommy, but until then, I get to care for adorable little guys like Tate."

Daisy laughed and nodded. "And let's be honest. You can't get much cuter than Tate."

"No, you can't," I agreed.

Although, a kid with Nate would probably be a good challenge to that theory. I hid a smile and looked up at Daisy again. "Thanks again for this. It means so much."

I sipped the last of my drink and glanced at the time.

"I should probably get going. A leprechaun is picking me up for an Irish dinner out in approximately fifteen minutes."

"Does he wear a cowboy hat, by any chance?" Abby teased.

"Sometimes."

Daisy laughed. "Tell Nate I said hi."

I chuckled, standing up before bending over to give Tate a little peck on the cheek. Since I interrupted his lovefest with the muffin, he swatted me away.

"Text or call if you need anything, Daisy."

"Will do. Have fun tonight, and don't do anything I wouldn't do," she sang after me.

I smiled, opening the door and stepping out into the evening air. The temperature was in that odd moment of time when it didn't know whether it wanted to be winter or spring. The temperatures tonight were going to drop into the twenties even though it almost hit fifty this afternoon. I thought about Nate and my heart skipped a beat.

That was the problem. The mere thought of him got me excited and hopeful, but I had to listen to my heart and my mind equally this time. I'd made progress when it came to Leo, which happened because of Nate. If it weren't for him, I wasn't sure I would have been able to process the obvious discrepancies in my logic about small towns.

But if I were to think about something long-term with Nate, and at my age, my mind went there automatically, I needed more. And I was at that stage because I knew my heart was about to fall heavily and fast for Nate.

As I pulled down the street to the house, I saw Nate's SUV already in the drive. He was leaning against the hood, looking sexy as hell.

It was as if all logic flew out the window, and I tapped my horn lightly.

Tonight was about green beer and maybe even getting lucky.

The rest could wait.

I pulled in next to his SUV, and he pushed himself off the vehicle and walked over to my driver's side, opening the door as I grabbed my purse.

"You look sensational," he said, helping me out of my car.

"Really? Have you started drinking early?" I teased.

"Only caffeine." He slid his arms around my waist and pulled me close, his eyes staying on mine as I drew a deep breath. "I've missed you."

I nodded, feeling the strength in his embrace. "I've missed you too, Sheriff."

He pressed his mouth against mine, swiping his

tongue along my lips, which I eagerly parted. His fingers tangled in my hair, and I let out a happy moan before breaking away.

"I could kiss you all night," I said softly.

"That's my hope." He curled his fingers around mine, holding my hand as we made our way to the house. I let go and opened the door, kicking off my shoes and putting my purse down.

"I'll go freshen up, and I'll be right out," I said, swiping a quick kiss across his lips.

He snagged my wrists and smiled, pulling me in. "One more."

The electricity buzzing between us was sharp and impossible to ignore. He cupped my face gently and kissed me again. I could feel my impatience to sleep with him knocking so heavily on my heart. The throbbing of his lips against mine, the whimper of moans escaping my lips, just everything about him made me want that next level.

We needed that next level.

I took a deep breath in and stepped back, our mouths barely parting until I pushed against his chest.

His eyes opened, and the familiar smirk fell across his expression.

"I'm hungry. I want some corned beef and cabbage."

I spun around and made my way to the bedroom, a part of me hoping he'd follow and the other party praying he didn't. I called over my shoulder, "I'll be right back."

"I'll be waiting, Amy."

My heart squeezed when he said my name, and I knew how much I loved being around Nate. Every single thing about him drove me wild. Even just hearing *Amy…*

By the time I got into my room, I collapsed on the bed and wondered how I'd be able to reconcile what my heart craved versus what my mind demanded.

Chapter Twenty-Two

Nate

Something was off on St. Paddy's Day. The chemistry was on fire. Her sweetness coated every part of me and made me crave more.

But there was something else going on, and I couldn't figure out what.

It worried me.

And I hadn't heard from her for a few days.

That concerned me even more.

She was helping out with Tate but usually still found time to slide into my text messages.

Amy had mentioned she'd booked a room at the Honey Leaf Lodge this week, but I didn't know which day. I'd asked in the mix of other texts, and I never got the date.

Not to mention, I'd been extremely busy with spring planning for our department. As warmer weather rolled in, our needs changed, and concerns turned more to water than the icy streets we had to patrol.

But as I sat down at my computer in my cramped office, I knew what I needed to do first and foremost.

The screen's glow seemed harmless in my office's dim light, the sun already setting outside. There was something unsettling washing over me, and I knew what I needed to do.

I hovered over Tom's message, worried that the email would bring news that would unravel me and freeze me with uncertainty. The subject line told me that he didn't want to write whatever he'd written, which made me not want to read it even more.

The implications of the message could pull me right back to that night or fling me carelessly forward into a future I wasn't ready for.

The thought of telling Amy about my friendship's demise made me spiral down a rabbit hole I'd rather not dive into. I'd carefully constructed a façade of strength and resilience. I helped others. They didn't have to help me. I ensured the spotlight veered away from my own inner demons because I wasn't sure I was strong enough to face them.

I'd always thought time would heal or at least buffer

the reality of what happened. I'd hoped that for Tom, too.

My best friend since grade school.

But judging by the subject line, it hadn't.

And if I were to dig deep, I expected that.

With every passing second, it felt like, layer by layer, my nightmare was unfolding and peeling back the painful memories.

I sat immobilized for what felt like hours with an unrelenting anxiety that threatened to crush me, but I had to do it. I had to face whatever words he or his family had for me.

When I clicked the email, it opened right up, filling my screen with a far-reaching message containing little but animosity.

The first sentence blared a scathing reminder of what he thought about me and the town we'd both grown up in. The next line appeared to be equally as angry.

And I didn't blame him.

I wouldn't.

I kept reading, and my heart sank lower, deeper into my gut as the dream of a reconciliation disintegrated with each word.

But I understood.

I always would.

As I hit the last paragraph, I let out a deep sigh and closed my eyes, letting the tears edge my eyelids as I pressed my fingers along my lashes to wipe away the wetness. I sniffed in the next batch of tears and blinked my eyes open.

Had I just responded to her positively...

I cleared my throat as my eyes fell to the last paragraph and let out a deep, steady breath. Each word was succinct in meaning with a clipped tone and an even more direct message, but the last sentence surprised me.

Turned around the message.

And created an inner turmoil that rocked my world and everything I knew about forgiveness and second chances.

That might have been my problem. I'd always wanted to hold onto that hope and believe in them.

I didn't like that side of me that believed in fairy tales like those because that was precisely what it was—a belief in the implausible.

Not every story ended happily.

Not every human had a happy ever after.

And I was the least of those who deserved one.

I reached for my cold cup of coffee and took a sip as I stared at the email, which was begging for a reply. With every tap of the keyboard, I prayed that this message would be received with the positive intention I meant.

In the first line, I apologized.

The second, I asked for forgiveness.

In the third sentence, I granted them their wish.

The fourth line, I told Tom that a day never went by that I didn't think of Ella, him, or his family.

Finally, I told him I'd be in touch with details, and I signed off.

My hands shook with pent-up emotion threatening my own stability. Without realizing it, I crumpled into the man I'd tried so hard to hide.

All it took was my careless response to destroy an entire family.

The ache in my chest worsened with every passing minute, and I knew I needed the one woman who could understand me. I turned off my computer, grabbed my things, and got into my SUV. The low hum of the radio did little to drown out the thoughts I had churning through my mind over and over again. It felt like my mind was on an endless loop, replaying all the things I could have done differently.

This.

This was why I'd stopped thinking about much other than my job.

If I allowed my mind freedom to think, it went to places I didn't want it to go.

I drove to Amy's, parked, and walked up to the front door. Hesitating a few seconds, I finally knocked. I waited a few minutes and then rang the doorbell. Leaning against the doorframe for strength, I prayed she'd answer.

Amy was the one light I had right now. My parents didn't need to see me like this. I didn't want them to needlessly worry.

But I knew Amy. Amy wouldn't judge me.

She wouldn't ask questions. She'd just let me be me. That was all I wanted right now.

Her familiar voice floated through the door.

"Who is it?"

"Nate."

Amy opened the door quickly, and I straightened.

"Nate, you look like hell. Are you okay?" Her eyes scanned me up and down before ushering me inside. "Seriously, Nate. What's going on? You look... awful."

"I feel even worse," I mumbled, spotting a suitcase by the door. "You going somewhere?"

She nodded. "Headed over to Honey Leaf Lodge."

"Ah, I wondered when you planned that."

"Tonight seemed like as good a night as any." She reached over with her hands and rubbed my arms up and down like I'd just entered from a blizzard. It was oddly comforting.

"You want to talk about it?"

I sucked on my bottom lip for a second and shook my head.

"Of course not," she muttered, taking a breath. "Can I get you something to drink?"

I shook my head, realizing I was about to interrupt the one moment away she had.

"Sorry. I just had a rough day," I told her. "I just wanted to see your face. You always make things better."

She smiled and nodded. "Talking about things might help, too."

"I know, but..."

Disappointment darted through her eyes. "Why don't you have a seat?" Amy pulled me to the couch and sat next to me. "What's going on?"

"A lot. It's all mental stuff I just have to work through." I sat down and looked over at her. She was gorgeous. Her hair loosely fell below her shoulders. The pink cashmere sweater hugged her body in all the right ways. And her heart was completely open. I could feel that from her. I looked away before bringing my gaze back.

Her lips pressed into a frown. "Anything that tears you up this badly isn't something you should just dismiss."

"I'm not dismissing it. I'm just uncomfortable talking

about it. Honestly, I thought coming here, I wouldn't have to."

She looked puzzled. "Why's that?"

I steepled my fingers and leaned over, shaking my head. "It's just stuff from a long time ago, and I don't think bringing you into it would help the issue."

"Wow. Okay." She scooted a little farther away. "You don't trust me or…"

My eyes flashed to hers, and panic set in. "No. It's not like that at all. I trust you with all my heart."

"Then why not tell me? It wasn't like it was easy to open up about Leo. I was embarrassed and worried." She let out a deep breath. "But I did it, and it was the best decision I'd made since coming here."

"And I thank you for telling me." I nodded.

"But don't you see how maybe I want to be included in your world too? I just don't see this going very far if communication doesn't go both ways."

I nodded in agreement. "No, I get it. I do. I see where you're coming from, and I do need to tell you more things."

"Why not start with what's bothering you today?"

I shook my head. "I can't do that. It's too complicated and—"

She let out a frustrated grunt and tucked her leg underneath her. "I don't get it, Nate. I really don't. This whole tough guy thing only works for so long."

I laughed, shaking my head. The discomfort rolled through me as her eyes stayed on mine. "I'm not a tough guy."

She came closer and rested her hand on my knee, letting out her breath slowly. "I like you, Nate. I'm pretty sure you like me, too."

"More than you know."

"Then show me. Open up to me."

"I'm trying, Amy. I really am." Her eyes stayed on mine, but I could see that I wasn't giving enough by the look in her eyes.

"You came here to feel better, but without having to tell me." She folded her arms over her chest. "Then, fine. I'll give you that luxury this one time, but if you want this to work, you need to start opening up to me. I can't be the only one giving. I've done that too many times, and I refuse to do it again."

Her words hit me hard because they were true.

And I would start opening up to her.

Just not today. Not about this.

I nodded. "I know. I'm just... Listen, I'm feeling better already. Go and enjoy your night away. We'll talk when you get back. You deserve this break more than anyone."

"No," she said, grabbing my hand and cupping it

between both of hers.

Amy looked into my eyes and let out a slow breath. "How about you come with me?"

"To the lodge?"

She nodded. "How about it?"

"But it's meant for you to relax and..." I stood, readying to leave.

"I'm not much for relaxing." She squeezed my hand and winked at me. "Come on, what do you say? Please?"

She stood on her tippy toes and smiled, brushing her nose against mine. "You never know what could happen?"

"Is that so?" I said, pulling her close.

My arms wrapped around her waist as she nodded, looking dreamily into my eyes.

"My day might have just gotten a whole lot better."

She tilted her head up and smiled wider. "I hope so. I've missed you."

"I've missed you too."

Amy took a step back and spun around, looking at her suitcase. "You ready, then? Is your answer yes?"

I nodded. "Should I swing by the house and grab some clothes?"

A coy look darted through her gaze. Her mouth curled slightly on the right.

Damn. She was sexy, and she didn't deserve to have to deal with my crap.

"I wouldn't bother." She winked at me. "What time do you have to be in tomorrow?"

I shook my head. "I don't. I have the day off."

"It's meant to be," she said, nodding. "See how life works out?"

I laughed. "I'm beginning to. One of the deputies needed Saturday off, so I traded with him."

Was it truly a coincidence? I thought about the mule. The Christmas party months ago. How I'd been thrown into Amy's orbit more than once.

Nah. The mule was just Lucky being lucky.

"What's got you *finally* grinning?" she asked, grabbing her small suitcase.

"You," I said simply as I kissed her again and hoped I didn't lose the best thing I had going for me.

Chapter Twenty-Three

Amy

I knew that Nate was hurting and I wanted to make him better, but I wasn't sure how to do it. I couldn't force the man to talk to me about things that were on his mind.

Glancing out the window, I let out a little breath of frustration as I looked to see the narrow path winding through the towering pines, which were swaying with the gentle breeze and casting shadows onto the mostly snowless ground. With the warmer temperatures, the ice dripped into puddles, and the snow melted into the ground.

It would be fun to spend springtime around Buttercup Lake. It would definitely provide a different perspective. I'd only known this little town in the frigid winter temperatures, bundled up like a walking, talking marshmallow.

But I couldn't shake the disappointment from earlier. Nate looked miserable, and he wouldn't even give me a hint of what made him that way. His spirits had turned around since the house, but that didn't change the fact that I still knew absolutely nothing about his worries.

I knew what it was like to open my heart and be vulnerable. I was scared, but Nate made me feel like I could tell him anything, and it worried me that I hadn't made Nate feel that comfortable.

The lodge finally came into view with its glowing lights dotting the exterior, peeping from between the log cabin façade and the large wraparound porch. The place was tucked away in a clearing, surrounded by pine trees left over from the mill days. I glanced around and couldn't spot where the petting zoo was for the farm animals, but it was dark outside.

I'd gotten so used to the snow reflecting moonlight that I'd forgotten that when the sun sets, it was hard to see. Nate glanced at me and smiled.

"Now, you're sure about this? I can just drop you off and pick you up tomorrow."

I laughed and shook my head, seeing the kindness bathing his expression. "And then what would I do with myself?"

He smiled and nodded, pulling into a parking spot in

the gravel lot.

"It's a great place they have here," he said, turning off the vehicle.

"You've been here?"

"I've been just about everywhere."

I chuckled and nodded. "I guess that would make sense, considering what you do for a living."

I turned to look at Nate, and his eyes were already on me. A charge bolted between us in the small space of the vehicle, and my breath caught.

He brought his thumb up slowly and brushed it along my lips. "I didn't mean to hurt your feelings, Amy."

I nodded, knowing in my heart that was true. "Let's make the most of tonight, and we'll see where things lead."

Nate's smile widened. "Sounds like a plan I can get behind."

He got out of the car and walked over to my side, helping me out before I could unbuckle from the seat as he looped his fingers through mine.

Nate grabbed my bag with his other hand, and we walked hand in hand toward the lodge. The heavy wooden door felt solid as Nate pushed it open to reveal a welcoming lobby with a large fireplace where flames crackled in the corner and a cozy reading nook stuffed with stacks of paperbacks.

"Good evening."

I glanced over to see a woman behind the counter smiling at us. Nate gave a quick nod and smiled as I made my way over to check-in.

"I'm Fiona," she said warmly. "If you need anything at all during your stay, let me or one of the staff know, and we'll do our best."

Her eyes narrowed at Nate. "Aren't you the sheriff?"

I chuckled. It was like I was dating a local celebrity.

"I am." He smiled. "And you're Fifi. I remember calling about the escaped mule."

"Ah, yes. Did you ever catch the four-legged Houdini?" she teased.

She typed into the laptop as I handed over the gift card.

"Yeah. I did, and she's now living at my house."

Fifi grinned. "Sounds about right. The animals here just make themselves at home."

She slid a card over for our room and gave us quick directions to get there. Several buildings with more rooms were behind this one, but ours was in the main lodge.

Nate squeezed my hand gently as we turned and made our way to a grand staircase encased with beautiful log carvings. He glanced at me, and my heart raced a little at the thought of what tonight might hold.

By the time we made it to the landing, he snuck another look in my direction, and I chuckled.

"What?" I asked.

"You just make me feel so... alive... and good." He stopped walking only a few doors away from our room and pulled me into him.

"I feel the same about you," I said softly, looking into his eyes.

My heart pounded a little harder as his eyes dropped to my mouth, and he swept a soft kiss along my lips before we got to the room.

It was like he could see the most private parts of me before I even revealed them. My stomach knotted with anticipation as I slid the card through the lock and pushed open the door to reveal a bucket of champagne and strawberries.

Nate eyed me. "Did you order this for yourself?"

I laughed and shook my head. "No, but there's a card."

He put the suitcase near the wall as I lifted the note to read,

Nate's off tomorrow, and the strawberries won't eat themselves, and there's far too much champagne to drink by yourself. We'd be worried about you all night. He's probably just staring at Lucky, anyway. Hugs, TSBC

"Those buggers," I said, glancing at Nate as I put the card down. "They planned this."

"They couldn't have known I'd be with you."

I smiled. "No, but they were the ones who had your officer ask to swap days."

"There is no winning with those ladies," he said, smiling and looping his arms around my waist.

"I have to confess that I don't mind one bit."

The air in the room was charged with tension as he took a step closer, completely eliminating the space between us.

His eyes stormed with desire as my pulse raced with anticipation. I'd wanted to take this step with Nate for so long, and now, here it was.

Nate leaned forward and dragged his mouth against mine, teasing me slightly as my eyes closed and my body pressed against his.

I felt the hardness of his abs and everything else moving against me as our kisses deepened. His mouth tasted so good. His hands ran down my spine as I nipped at his bottom lip. An amused chuckle rolled off his lips before being replaced with a satisfied growl of need.

He broke his mouth away from mine and took a step back as my arms fell to my side, unsure of what to do next, but I didn't have to wait. He pulled off his shirt, kicked off his jeans, and came back for another kiss before running his fingers under my sweater, helping it over my head.

Nate's mouth pressed along my skin, skimming over the lace of my bra as the stubble of his chin tickled me. My fingers pushed through his hair as his hands worked to unfasten my bra. It slid to the floor as his lips covered my nipple while his fingers worked to tease the other.

Warmth pooled in my belly as the slickness of his tongue ran along my skin and his fingers undid my jeans. I shimmied out of them quickly as his mouth met mine once more. His tongue darted into my mouth as his palm cupped my underwear, the dampness spreading.

Everything about tonight felt amazing and right. The worries from earlier drifted away, and I kissed him harder. He stepped back and glanced at the champagne and walked over to the table, pulling it out of the ice bucket. He set the strawberries on the bed, popped the cork off the champagne, and poured some into the flutes.

Nate slowly pushed me back against the bed, carefully pouring the cold liquid onto my belly. Goosebumps spread across me. His lips followed the trail of champagne, which led to my underwear. His fingers quickly worked to move them down as his mouth continued to follow the path.

My finger hooked along the elastic of his underwear, and I rolled down one side.

"A little impatient?" he teased, helping them all the way off as I kicked my own from my ankles.

Nate towered over me, every part of him hard and toned as he kneeled in front of me, moving his mouth slowly across my thighs, following my curves.

I ground my hips toward him as he looked up, locking eyes with me. I sucked on my bottom lip for a brief moment before he climbed on top of me, peppering my neck with kisses as his fingers moved between my thighs.

My entire body squirmed from the desire running through me. It was impossible to hide the eagerness I felt for him to be inside me. I looped my arms around his neck when his mouth found mine, and a moan hummed from my mouth as I pushed my hips into him.

I could feel him smile through our kisses as he spread my legs with his knees, sliding into me with a fullness that felt out of this world. Heat lashed through me as he pushed into me deeper, and my fingers dug into his back.

He let out a growl of appreciation as I rolled my hips into him in our own rhythmic dance. He stopped and started kissing along my collarbone, down my breasts to my belly, as his mouth felt the warmth between my legs.

With every lash of his tongue, my mind went crazy numb as my nails ran along his hair, and another moan left my lips. Nate's mouth slowly moved along my belly until he moved on top of me again. My pulse pounded with heat and anticipation like never before as he slid into me again. His mouth crashed to mine as my tongue willingly met his.

My hips wiggled as he pushed deeper into me. It was like I was teetering on a tightrope, about to fall... but I didn't know if there was anything to catch me.

"Wait," I whispered breathlessly. "I don't want this to end."

He slowed his hips and braced himself over me, hovering as his eyes locked on mine. "It won't end. It's only the beginning."

Nate kissed the top of my nose and moved his mouth to mine. His fingers pressed and rubbed between my legs while my thighs squeezed into him, and my world exploded with his. Every cell in my body felt like it was on fire and pulsing with something I craved from him.

And I needed so much more.

My body arched into his as Nate's arms held me tightly, and I knew that my heart belonged to him, even if only for tonight.

Chapter Twenty-Four

Nate

Timing.

Timing was everything, and Amy had already flown to Chicago to help with her sister's engagement.

It was bittersweet. We'd made that push forward to something more. Something that might last.

But an unsettled feeling moved in the moment she'd left four days ago.

And I knew why.

She'd have time away to reflect on things, on me, on us.

And the fact that I wasn't letting her in, or at least that was how she felt, only made me more paranoid.

I sat in my office and glanced at my inbox, wishing

the emails would answer themselves. All I truly wanted to do was go to Amy and apologize, let her in on what's been haunting me, and hope…

It wasn't my place, though. Tonight was the night that Alice's boyfriend was going to propose, and I didn't need to interrupt anything.

This moment for all of them was important. I knew that Amy adored George and thought he was perfect for Alice. I didn't need to be the inconsiderate guy who didn't know when to keep his mouth shut.

I tapped my finger on the table and pushed away from my desk. I had some investigating of my own to do, and it started with Millie.

According to Grace, the doctor had allowed Millie to resume all previous activities, so I felt it would be okay to stop by the coffee shop in a bit and ask some questions. Grace had mentioned she was meeting her grandma there around two, so I had about fifteen minutes to get there.

I grabbed my keys and walked out to see Flo knitting some socks. I chuckled. "Slow day?"

"Aren't they always?" she asked, setting down the red yarn. "I thought today was an office day."

"It has been, but I'm gonna go grab some coffee. Want anything?"

"No. I'm plenty full on energy."

"Okay, see ya in a bit," I told her, walking out of the building.

The temperature was downright balmy. It had to be in the fifties at the coldest. A red cardinal bolted from a branch hanging over my vehicle and landed on the tree next to me. It was hard to beat the seasons here in Wisconsin. Some might think we had brutal winters, but the truth was that we had deep seasons. The sweetness of the fall leaves hung in the air long enough to greet the snow falling on the ground, and when springtime came, the blue skies made way for gentle breezes determined to push out the clouds and welcome in the tiny buds on all the trees. Once summer hit, the warmth felt great and the humidity welcomed, and it stuck around just long enough to get a person excited for fall again.

It was a cycle.

It's kind of like the Sunshine Breakfast Club. They'd find their target, coerce, propel, and finally congratulate one single person at a time.

As I pulled across the street from the coffee shop, I glanced around the town and sighed disappointedly. Just knowing Amy wasn't in town made this place a little less cheerful and my heart a lot less happy.

There was no doubt about it. The book club's ability

to match two people was uncanny, and I truly believed it all started from the heart of one person.

I walked across the street and opened the door to the coffee shop. The aroma of fresh-ground coffee beans permeated the air as I spotted Millie with Grace by the fireplace. She looked as good as new again.

Abby smiled. "How are you doing this fine day, Sheriff?"

I narrowed my eyes on her. "I'm doing well. How about yourself?"

"Great. So, how'd the Honey Leaf Lodge treat you the other night?"

"An Americano, iced, in a large cup sounds perfect, Abby. Thanks for asking."

She snickered as I shook my head, knowing full well that each and every member had been involved in shoving Amy and me together.

And it all started with that damn mule.

Lucky.

"Here you go, Nate." Abby handed me the drink, and I smiled.

"Thanks, Abby," I called over my shoulder as I made my way to Millie and Grace.

"Good to see you up and at 'em, Millie," I said,

sliding a chair over to their table.

Grace kept in a giggle and glanced at her grandma.

"It's better than the alternative."

"Agreed." I nodded and took a sip. "Now that you're feeling better, I do have some questions for you, though."

Millie's eyes widened. "Am I in trouble, Sheriff?"

I kept my face expressionless. "Yet to be seen."

She clutched her shirt collar and laughed. "Oh, dear."

Millie had a beauty in her gaze held together by an infinite wisdom lent to her from years on this earth. The fine lines that framed her eyes smoothed into rosy cheeks with a few pieces of white hair hanging along her jaw that escaped the hair clip.

"This sounds serious," she said, picking up her tea and taking a sip.

"Let's start with the call you made about a runaway mule," I said flatly, opening my small tablet to make notes.

Millie offered a small, knowing smile as she kept her eyes on me. She was preparing to go toe-to-toe with me. Her silver brows arched. "What about it?"

"Where did you first see this mule?"

She chuckled. "Does it really matter now? She's roaming the pastures in your back yard the last I heard."

"It does matter. We need to ensure public resources

aren't wasted."

A twinkle in her gaze lent to a pseudo frown as she glanced at her granddaughter. "Like I reported, I saw the mule walking straight into Nick and Brielle's yard. You know, the house across the street and down a few from Hunter and Daisy."

"I know the house."

She chuckled and took another sip of tea and set it down. "Of course you do, Sheriff. Very well, if I'm hearing correctly."

"Not sure where you're headed with that one, Millie." I cleared my throat. "What exactly was the mule doing when you saw it walking into the yard?"

"Well, it looked cold." She pretended to shiver. "And it looked lost, very lost."

"Right." I glanced at Grace, who was staring at the ceiling. "And you'd heard about the missing mule from the petting zoo, right, Millie?"

She nodded. "That's right."

"And you needed to add credibility to your first call."

She laughed. "Why would I need to do that?"

"Well, Millie." I ran my finger along the notepad and took a sip of my drink. "Because the person calling in about the missing mule from the petting zoo was anonymous... and false."

"But…" She closed her mouth and looked worriedly at her granddaughter.

"There was no missing mule from Honey Leaf Lodge, and that second report had been anonymous. You made both of those calls, didn't you?"

She refused to look at me.

"You made a false statement to an officer, Millie," I said. "That's not good."

Her chin tilted up, and her eyes met mine. "But it was worth it, wasn't it, Sheriff Nate?"

She had me there.

"So, what are you going to do about this, Nate?" Grace asked.

"I think the Sunshine Breakfast Club has gotten ahead of itself. It's not above the law, Millie. You're not above the law. I can't have false statements flooding our non-emergency line."

Millie chuckled. "Talk to my lawyer."

"Millie, you can't go around messing with emergency services just so you can hook up two people. I've always turned the other way, but I can't this time."

Millie's expression remained unchanged. "Why's that?"

Encouraged by her response, I leaned forward. "Because I can't afford to feed more than one mule, Millie."

Her shoulders relaxed. "You're not really mad. Are you, Nate?"

"Not in the slightest." I wiped my hands along my pants and let out a sigh. "But I'm in a pickle thanks to you."

She touched her chest and scowled. "Me?"

I nodded. "Yeah, you see…"

"What?" Grace prodded.

"I'm falling in love with a woman at the very same time that I'm screwing it all up with her."

Millie and Grace traded a look.

"And I blame you for that. The whole club, really." My knee bobbed up and down before I stretched my legs.

"If you know you're screwing things up, why aren't you fixing them?" Millie asked.

"It's not that easy."

"Love isn't that hard," Millie countered.

I frowned. "Do you always have an answer for everything?"

"I do." She laughed. "It's the one benefit of getting old. That and I have resources." A smug look slid across Millie's face.

"Yeah, well…" I squinted my eyes at her. "Wait a

second. Millie, this isn't funny."

She looked puzzled. "What?"

"Where did you get that mule? It's one thing to waste my department's time, but you can't go stealing livestock."

Millie gasped and Grace snickered. "I'd never go stealing animals. What kind of weirdo do you think I am?"

"Millie, where did she come from?"

"I don't know what you're talking about."

I cocked my head slightly and stayed silent. "You know, the poor Mule almost bit the dust. You can't just let animals free to roam in the middle of winter."

"Had you done your job, Sheriff, and not gotten distracted by a pair of breasts, you would have found the mule on their property." Millie straightened. "I'd tied her up on the side of the house, but you took so long, you must have missed her, and then she got free. When I saw the mess you were getting yourself into, I went and grabbed a coffee. When I came back, the mule was missing and so were you. I even left to give you two privacy."

As I stared at this woman in front of me, I realized there was no getting through to her. She wouldn't see the many issues riddled through this entire scenario. I mean, I didn't even know where to begin.

"Where did she come from, Millie?"

"Amy or the mule?" She flashed a wry grin, and I just stared at her, trying not to laugh.

"Fine. You're no fun. I know a guy a few towns over. He let me buy her for a good deal because she's such a headache. I picked her up around Valentine's Day."

I knew there was more to the story.

"And?"

"And I got a few of the guys at the department to steal some of your things so she could snuggle up to them."

I thought back to what Amy had said about imprinting.

"Why would you do that?"

She let out a deep sigh. "Honestly, Nate… I figured if you screwed things up with Amy, at least you'd have a mule who loved you." She looked over at her granddaughter. "And by the looks of it, I made a good decision."

There was nothing good about any of this.

"Listen, I'm rooting for you two. When Daisy came up with—"

"You're telling me all of this was Daisy's idea? So that means Hunter really has been in on it." I shook my head. "I'll be. Nothing is sacred in this town."

Grace laughed. "You're preaching to the choir."

"Ah, yes. You understand my plight."

Grace nodded. "I also understand when it's time to just give in."

"Give in to what?" I asked.

Grace looked at Millie for a second before turning her attention back to me. "Love."

I straightened in my chair and shifted slightly. "Love. It's not the love I'm worried about, Grace. It's that Amy deserves better."

Grace looked surprised. "Nate, you're as good as they come. You just… you just need to let down your guard a little."

"That's the one message I keep getting loud and clear."

Millie's white brows raised. "Amy mentioned it to you?"

I nodded. "Millie, I'll look the other way about the calls you made to the department, but I'd like you to do something for me in return."

She looked around the coffee shop and leaned forward. "What's that?"

I scraped my fingers along my jaw. I couldn't believe this was what all my years in law enforcement had led to. I stared at Millie and her granddaughter.

"I need the Sunshine Breakfast Club's help." I shook

my head. "I just hope I'm not too late."

Chapter Twenty-Five

Amy

The magnificent mile didn't feel so magnificent. Don't get me wrong. Seeing my sister accept George's proposal was what dreams were made of last night, but the moment I'd left Buttercup Lake, I wasn't sure I wanted to go back. And I had no idea where that thought came from since when I was there, I couldn't imagine leaving.

I looked up at the street, a sea of buildings stretching as far as the eye could see. The sidewalks bustled with people who didn't know me, and I could feel the comfort of being unnoticed washing over me again. The towering skyscrapers reflected the sun, spraying a shimmering glow along the buildings.

I usually loved wandering the sidewalks, peering into

the windows of stores I'd never afford while daydreaming about my future. The collection of shops and restaurants claimed a vibrancy that could only be found in a big city, but it wasn't vibrant from the people.

My stomach tensed when I thought about Buttercup Lake and the amazing people there, the book club, the little life I'd started building for myself.

The growth I'd had…

I followed the sidewalk away from the shopping and cafes to Brielle and Nick's place in the city. They'd kept Jill, one of the nannies, there and took one with them to Japan, but they had no problem with my staying there while I was in the city for my sister.

Opening the door to the townhome, I was met with the smell of chocolate chip cookies. There was something about that sugary, buttery goodness with a hint of chocolate that couldn't be mistaken.

"Those smell amazing, Jill," I called, sliding my shoes off.

I climbed up the stairs to the kitchen, where I saw a platter of chocolate chip cookies but no Jill. I was tempted to snag one, but I didn't want to take one in case she needed them for something. I let the familiarity coat my soul as I thought about my needs, but that was the problem. I didn't know what those were any longer.

Looking around, I couldn't help but notice how everything in Brielle and Nick's house was perfectly put together and styled. But there were moments when I wondered if it was just for show. Could things be that perfect all the time?

But this was what I'd become used to living with them, and it kind of skewed my reality. My hand slid along the exposed brick wall, which blended well with the paintings they'd displayed, while an oversized cobalt blue couch centered the room. Silver drapes swept down to the floor while every shelf was dusted, and books were put in their proper place.

The familiarity put a smile on my face as I climbed the stairs to where my bedroom was. The nannies each had a bedroom stationed on the same floor as Tate's, and then Brielle and Nick's bedroom was on the top floor.

It was a beautiful place.

I opened the door to my bedroom and fell back onto my bed, finally taking a deep breath from the whirlwind of activities since I'd arrived.

So much had happened in a short period of time that I didn't have a chance to worry about Nate—about us. But I knew without a shadow of a doubt that I felt so unsettled because I didn't know what to do.

It would be so easy to pick up my life right where I left off in Chicago. It might be with a different family, and I'd miss Tate immensely, but it would be the easy thing to do.

I could move on quietly, unnoticed.

Forget that I'd shared so much of myself with a place I fell for.

With a person I fell for even harder.

Because I couldn't let myself fall for a man who couldn't be vulnerable with me.

Who couldn't tell me what in life scared him.

What dreams he thought impossible.

I needed to know that the man I spent the rest of my life with wanted to peel back my layers and wanted me to do the same for him.

I didn't want to be the person he came to because he knew he didn't have to tell me anything.

Those words stung far harder than I realized. It wasn't until I'd come back to Chicago and let my hormones chill out that it dawned on me what he really meant.

He liked it with me because it was superficial, at least on his end. He didn't have to work for my affection. He'd lend an ear for me, but he didn't have to unbury his skeletons with me. Nate could just keep them buried until they put him in his grave.

I rested my arm over my eyes and felt the tears roll down my cheeks.

But it was too late.

I'd already fallen for Nate.

Hard.

In the beginning, I wondered why each smile he threw my way felt like a gift from him. And then, as time went on, I realized that it was one. Seeing a genuine smile that touched his eyes as he looked at me made me feel like the luckiest woman in the world.

The problem was that he managed to divert conversations from the landscape of his feelings and drive them toward mine when I could feel a quiet storm raging inside him. He thought he could hide it from me, but I knew.

I could tell when his voice's timbre changed slightly when his childhood friend was brought up.

I felt the reluctance he had when I guided the conversation to his past, his hurt.

The irony didn't escape me. I'd been my most vulnerable with him, and it wasn't returned.

If anything, it felt like he'd closed up more.

And I'd fallen in love with him.

Or the idea of him.

I sniffled and wiped my eyes with my sleeve.

"Don't be ridiculous, Amy," I muttered to myself.

I'd only slept with him once. It wasn't like my entire life hinged on getting this man to be my forever. It wasn't like that.

I shook my head, knowing that wasn't true. It had nothing to do with sleeping with him and everything to do with the moment he'd knocked down my walls.

The moment I was no longer worried about showing where I came from and what I'd overcome.

I sat up and walked over to the window. The city moved on. It didn't keep tabs on me. I could continue on the same path, or I could blend right in with everyone else again.

I wasn't missed here, and that had an appeal.

And then it dawned on me. Nate prided himself on being rational.

The nerve.

But love was not rational. It was the most irrational emotion out there, and it wasn't just an emotion.

Love offered solace, preservation, protection, loyalty, and comfort. It could ground us or make us soar.

Love could also bring discomfort, pain, dishonesty, and an inability to protect ourselves, but that was when we lost it.

292

I let out a deep sigh, knowing that I loved Nate deeply and that I could love him even more if he let me in.

But my silent nightmare was that if we stayed together and he didn't let me in, the bridge we had keeping us together would slowly crumble away.

We'd be left with an emptiness between us where conversations stopped flowing, where he retreated inside himself and the strain of loving him hurt more than leaving him.

That thought scared me most of all. With moments of clarity like this, I knew that the safe thing to do was to stay in Chicago. I didn't want my emotions to change abruptly and wildly like the seasons in the Midwest. I needed stability. If anything, my childhood taught me that I was someone who wanted steadiness, commitment, and reciprocation.

I'd spent my childhood in search of all those things. I'd wanted so badly for my parents to love me how they would have loved sons. I wanted them to commit to me like they did their bad habits.

Nate offered me two of those things—stability and commitment. But I needed him to reciprocate. I needed Nate to give himself fully to me, and I shouldn't have to ask for it.

I knew the longer I stayed in the middle of a city that didn't notice me, the easier it would be to stay. I just hoped there would be someone to beg me to leave.

If nothing else, it was late afternoon, and I could pull on some pajamas, grab a book, and treat this like a vacation until I truly had to make a decision.

A soft knock on my door broke me out of my endless loop.

"Come in," I said, looking over.

"It's Jill, and I come bearing cookies and milk."

Jill appeared holding a plate with several cookies stacked high.

"How did the shopping go?" she asked, setting the plate on a desk.

"Not as well as I'd hoped. My chip malfunctioned, so my debit didn't work."

Jill rolled her eyes and chuckled. "Probably for the better. It saves you money."

"So true." I reached for a cookie and a glass of milk and sat on my bed, tapping the edge for her.

"Tell me all about Wisconsin. I only went there once right before Christmas to help unpack."

"Oh, yeah. That's right."

"Well, it's beautiful... quiet." I thought about the little town I grew so fond of. "The people are great. It's beautiful in the winter, so I can only imagine what it's like in the summer." I stopped myself.

She kept her eyes on me and waited a few seconds. "But?"

I took a bite of the buttery cookie to buy myself time. "But I'm not sure it's for me. Everyone knows everything. There are no secrets. There's nowhere to hide."

She snickered.

"And they have a real farm animal crisis. Things are getting loose all the time. Do you realize some lady lost her chicken, and it wound up on the local news?"

Jill smiled with a wistful look in her eyes. "Better than what's on our news."

She had a point.

"It's a simpler life," I said more to myself than Jill. I reached for another cookie. "These are amazing."

"Thank you, but I miss your cherry pie."

"I'll make some before I leave and stick them in the freezer."

"Promise?"

I nodded, thinking about going back. Daisy and Hunter told me to take a few weeks off and enjoy Chicago and my sister. So far, that's what I intended to do. And think about Nate and me.

A lot.

"Have you made friends? Met any cute guys?" she teased.

I chuckled. "Yes, and yes."

Her brows arched in surprise. "Seriously?"

"I even belong to a book club."

She waved her hands around and shook her head. "I don't want to hear about books. I want to hear about the men."

"It's not men. It's just one man, and he's incredible." I took another bite of the cookie. "But I'm not sure much will come of it."

"Don't say that." She shook her head. "Have confidence in things."

My phone rang, and it was some 800 number. I debated about answering but decided to pick up.

The moment the woman said she was from my bank, my heart dropped.

It wasn't a chip malfunction.

The customer service rep started rattling off charges, none of which were mine, and my heart sank. My entire savings was gone. I'd never opened a savings account, just an interest earning checking account.

I felt sick. Sweat pricked my forehead.

"What's wrong?" Jill mouthed.

The woman finally asked me if the charges were

legitimate, and if we should stop the card.

It felt like the world was spinning. With room and board covered for so many years, I'd managed to save up a lot.

Well, a lot for me. Maybe not Brielle and Nick a lot… But…

It was gone.

A lump in the back of my throat only grew as the woman rattled off the investigation they were opening—how long it would be before I saw my money again, if I saw my money again, and the forms they were emailing.

Everything turned to slow motion. I didn't even have enough money to rent a car and drive back to Buttercup Lake or fly in on the putter plane.

I hung up the phone in a state of shock as Jill pieced it together.

But the worst thing about it all was that I knew who did it, and I realized it wasn't Nick and Brielle's money Leo was after. It had been mine.

Chapter Twenty-Six

Nate

I rolled my shoulders back and took a deep breath as I pulled into a parking garage. This could go a lot of different ways, and I wasn't sure I was ready for most of them.

But I knew something was off. Amy had been in Chicago for two weeks. The date she said she'd be back to Buttercup Lake came and went, and the texts I received from her were spotty at best. Being the guy, I thought sleeping with her had bonded us and made us closer, but it certainly didn't feel that way.

Every time I drove by Nick and Brielle's, I saw Amy's car in the driveway, and relief would wash over me, followed by worry.

Wasn't she where she belonged?

And if it were just a simple vacation to be with her sister, why didn't she text much or return my calls?

So, here I was, in the middle of Chicago, hoping I didn't stumble onto something I didn't want to see.

As I locked up my car and made my way down to the sidewalk, I glanced up at the tall buildings towering over the streets.

Yup, just like I remembered it.

I walked alongside the buildings until I found the right address and stood outside the black door with a silver knocker for several minutes.

Not much scared me in life, but I hadn't wanted much before, either.

Just as I raised my knuckles to knock, the door swung open, and a woman I didn't recognize stepped out. I glanced at the silver house numbers to ensure I was in the right place.

"Oh, umm." I stepped to the side.

She stopped and looked up at me. A small, cheeky grin appeared on her face.

"You're the sheriff."

I looked down at my jeans and pullover and brought my gaze back to hers.

She laughed. "Amy's crush."

I let out a sigh of relief and nodded. "Is she here?"

"Yeah. She is. I'm Jill, by the way, another nanny." She turned back around and hollered that Amy had a visitor.

My heart hammered in my chest as I heard Amy's footsteps trotting down the stairs.

When our eyes connected, it felt like the world slipped away.

Jill muttered something and wandered down the street as Amy slowly made her way to the door.

"I didn't know you were coming down here," she said, smiling.

"I've missed you so much, Amy."

She leaned against the door and nodded. "I've missed you too."

"Why are you here?" she asked, glancing down the sidewalk.

"Well, it's been pretty hard to get in touch with you."

Amy licked her lips and let out a slow, thoughtful breath. "I've been busy."

"I gathered that."

"I've had a lot on my mind, Nate." Her arms folded over her chest.

A protective stance.

This wasn't good.

"About me?" My eyes stayed locked on hers, and I

could feel the energy drifting between us.

She nodded. "About you. About us. About my future. Even Leo."

"You've been thinking about Leo?"

"I kind of had no choice."

I frowned. "What do you mean?"

Amy reached for me. "Why don't you come on in, and we can talk?"

I nodded as her small hands tugged on my shirt. I landed inside, and she closed the door behind me, careful to lock all three locks.

A little different from Buttercup Lake.

"Let's go upstairs."

I glanced at the sitting room on this level that was meticulously curated to view from the street. The drapes were wide open, and the red throw sprawled over the white chenille chaise. Books spread on shelves were color coordinated and nothing was out of place. It looked like a spread out of a magazine.

Following Amy up the flight of stairs to the next level felt like a Herculean task. Every second felt like an hour.

When we finally reached the top, I spotted the kitchen and another family room. The entire house felt sterile.

She spun around and nearly knocked into me, and all

I could think about was that last night with her, holding her body in my arms, feeling her warmth next to me. I smiled, hooked my arm around her waist, and slowly brought her into me.

Her gaze softened as she looked into my eyes.

"I'm glad you're here," she said quietly.

"I wasn't sure…" My voice trailed off.

She took a step back and walked into the kitchen. "Would you like anything to drink?"

I shook my head. "I'm fine."

She grabbed an orange for herself and peeled it, putting the sections on a plate.

I followed her to the open family room and took a seat in the wingback chair near the window.

"You've been on my mind constantly," I told her. "I've thought a lot about what you said."

Amy took a bite of the orange and didn't say anything.

"I'm sorry for ever making you think that I don't trust you or that I can't be myself around you." I looked out the window and brought my gaze back to hers.

She curled her legs under her and nodded slowly. "This time away has been good for me."

"Yeah?"

Amy nodded but said nothing else. I found myself twisting my fingers together and shaking my head.

"You know how I told you that you made me feel again?"

"I remember that."

"It's true, and part of that is because I know that I can reveal things to you, and you won't judge me. I just never put a mental time limit on it. I just knew... so, part of me didn't want to rush things or bring the mood down." I shook my head. "It wasn't that I didn't want to talk to you about the things on my mind. I just wasn't even done fully processing them myself."

She leaned forward and put her empty plate on the glass coffee table. "But don't you think that's where I can come in? That's what talking things over is for, to hash things out." She let out a groan and sat back on the couch. "Nate, I can't be the person in the relationship who gives and gives. I want to feel worthy of your words."

"Amy, you are worthy. You're more than worthy, and I came here to tell you that." I stood, walked over to the window, and looked down. "Amy, I don't want to lose you. I'm not here to tell you things just to try to prove something, but I'm genuinely here because I want to open up to you. I want you to see all the parts of my life that make up me. I've spent a lot of time trying to hide the things that made me who I am and changed my views on the world and friendship, but I don't want to do that anymore."

Amy stood behind me and placed her hand on my shoulder, letting out a deep breath. "Nate, that's all I ever wanted."

I spun around to see tears in Amy's eyes that she quickly dabbed away.

"Since we're sharing things," she started. "The real reason I'm still here is because I can't afford to get to Buttercup Lake until May's paycheck hits. I'm mortified for even having to say it—"

"What? Why wouldn't you just tell me?"

She sniffled and shrugged. "Long story."

"I'm here for it." I twisted my fingers with hers and held her hand tight as she pulled me to the couch and sat down.

"One word for you." She let go of my hand and held up one finger.

I cocked my head slightly.

"Leo."

Dread spiked through me. "What about Leo?"

"Somehow, he got my debit card info when he was in town and drained my account."

Anger bit at my spine, and I was glad he wasn't here

so I didn't lunge at him.

"Are you serious?"

"And I'll be getting my money back, but it has been a hassle." She rubbed her temples and groaned. "All of my money was in my checking account because it paid interest and I'd never bothered opening a savings."

"I'm so sorry. I just want to throttle that guy."

"You and me both." She leaned against the couch. "So, I took it as a sign that I needed to stay here and think about things. The moment I came back to Chicago, everything I loved about being here sprang into place. The anonymity, the hustle and bustle, easy access… Only this time, the longer I stayed, the worse I felt. I always thought I loved that nobody noticed me, but I actually hate it."

I didn't want to get too excited and was still trying to work through the surprise about Leo, so I just nodded.

"And I realized that I probably needed a big city in my twenties so I could just blend in and get my bearings, but that's not what I'm craving now."

"What are you craving?"

"You." She smiled coyly and ran her fingers along my leg. "And Lucky. The Sunshine Breakfast Club, Abby knowing the drink I like in the morning, the giving tree at the community center, your parents' U-pick cherry orchard I've yet to see. But I'm willing to give it all up if you can't open up to me."

I nodded. "Did you tell the bank and the authorities your suspicions about Leo?"

"Heck, yeah. I didn't think twice." She laughed, but the tone just sounded sad. "The awful part is that he wasn't even smart enough to get creative with it. He used my money to make all these purchases, which I'm guessing he just planned on hawking, but he used the address where he was staying."

"Seriously?"

She nodded. "I was stunned."

"He probably thought you'd cover for him."

"Ha," she blurted. "He thought wrong. I'm done rationalizing the irrational."

"Good." I nodded, thinking about Tom. I'd received another email from him, and this one had surprised me.

"So, you know how I told you that I understood about being so tight and protective with a childhood friend?"

"Yeah."

"And that I knew what it felt like to lose that friendship?"

She turned to face me and nodded.

"I had a best friend named Tom. We did everything

together. Kind of sounded like you and Leo."

Amy kept her gaze on me but didn't say anything.

"We started first grade together and were inseparable all the way into college." The knot in my stomach tightened. "He had a little sister named Ella, and as we got older, she kind of put herself in the mix a lot, but she was so much younger than us that she couldn't really keep up. But she was a good kid. Sweet girl."

Amy nodded.

"By the time she hit high school, Tom and I were already in college. I was oblivious. I had no idea she had a crush on me. I just thought it was innocent enough and didn't really play into it much because she was just in high school." I'd never once spoken these words aloud. I'd never rehashed the story to a soul. Those who'd been around it knew it. There was never a need. "I think Tom appreciated the fact that I wasn't some creep trying to take advantage of the situation too."

She squeezed my hand. "I bet."

A lump formed in my throat, nearly squeezing it shut. I looked away and let out a deep breath, but it didn't make me feel any better.

"We came home for a visit from college. It was around St. Paddy's Day. Tom and I had been drinking too much, and Ella showed up. She started hitting on me—like, not high school girl stuff. It was…" I shook my head. "It was really awkward, and I didn't know what to do. I thought I had been clear that she was like my little sister over the years."

"Oh, no." Amy shook her head.

"I remember every single thing about that night. Unlike this year, we had deep snowbanks, frigid temperatures night and day, and constant storm warnings, but it was Wisconsin. We're used to it."

Amy scooted closer.

"So, Ella came on super hard when Tom went to the bathroom. I remember turning toward her and putting my hands on her shoulders. She looked so hopeful as she stared into my eyes." I shook my head, feeling the tears tinge my lashes. I wiped them away. "I remember telling her I thought she was beautiful, smart, and witty. That she'd make a man so lucky someday, but I wasn't that guy. She needed to enjoy high school and find a boyfriend her own age."

Amy's expression didn't change. She just listened.

"Tom came back from the bathroom just as his sister tore out of the place. I told him what had happened, and I was kind of worried he'd be pissed, but he told me he appreciated it and that she had to get the idea out of her mind." I shook my head. "And that's kind of what I thought. Just a simple crush that I redirected back to high school. But she never made it home."

Amy gasped, pulling my hands into hers. "Oh, Nate."

I cleared my throat, thinking back to that horrible night.

The panic.

Dismay.

Worry.

Anger.

"My uncle found her car buried in a snowbank. She had an empty bottle of vodka on the seat. We never found out how she got that. From what it looked like, she froze to death. She'd texted her mom that she wasn't coming home yet and was hanging out with us, but it wasn't true. She'd sent that text after she'd left. I know she never meant to… I mean, I think she just passed out, and the temperatures were such that…"

Amy nodded. "Yeah."

My shoulders lowered, and I realized that the tension I'd been carrying around for over a decade was starting to disappear. The grief and guilt no longer felt like they were strangling me. I looked out the window.

"I regret ever telling her anything at all. I should have just let it play out naturally."

Amy shook her head and touched my chin, turning it so my eyes met hers. "It did play out naturally, Nate. And it's awful and horrid and a nightmare no family should have to face, but it isn't because of you."

"That's not how they took it. By the time the memorial service came around, Tom wasn't speaking to me. If we bumped into each other on campus, he acted like I wasn't there. His family moved out of Buttercup Lake and down to Arizona. And I just became numb to emotion. Just flat."

Amy nodded. "It's not your fault, Nate. And everyone is allowed to grieve how they must, but it wasn't fair of Tom to blame you. No one could have predicted what transpired that night. No one."

"I feel like it could have gone a different way, Amy. If I had just been more…"

"What? Receptive? And then you get in trouble for coming on to a high school kid?"

Amy slid close, keeping my hands in hers. "You did what should be done. You let her down as easily as possible in a respectful, private manner. Nobody could have predicted what happened next, and it's unfair that you've been carrying around this guilt for so long."

"I don't know. I deserve it. They lost their baby girl,

his little sister…"

"No." She shook her head. "You are not to blame, and until you understand that this isn't your fault, your heart isn't going to heal."

"I thought I'd done a pretty good job of compartmentalizing, but I got an email from him a while back. When everything happened, my uncle had planned a beautiful area in the park down on the lake, near the main street, to memorialize Ella. The family turned him and the city down." I shrugged. "Anyway, the email from Tom said that they'd reconsidered, and even though it had been more than a decade, did the offer still stand?"

"Oh, Nate. I'm so sorry." I shook my head. "It probably opened everything up again."

"It did, but that's okay. I get it. They lost someone in their lives who should still be with them. And I'm the reason."

She shook her head. "You don't know that. Nobody does. For all we know, you could have told her the opposite, and she still drank the vodka to celebrate. She was young. She just didn't know how much was too much."

"I wish I could see it that simply. Anyway, I wrote back to Tom that we'd always kept that place open for Ella, and I apologized."

Amy nodded.

"Before I left for here, I got another message from Tom."

My stomach sloshed with uncertainty as I drew a deep breath. "He wants to come up to Buttercup Lake to meet with me."

"Wow. Okay."

"And I just don't know what to do with all these emotions that I'm feeling."

Amy nodded, holding my hands in hers, and rested her head on my shoulder.

"Sit in those emotions and be grateful you're finally feeling them again. We'll work on the rest next." She looked into my eyes. "Together."

Chapter Twenty-Seven

Amy

It felt so good to be back in Buttercup Lake. Nate helped me pack up most of my things, and we drove up north a week ago. Brielle was in town to be with Tate, so I'd been needed much more than usual, which was fine with me.

Job security.

But this morning, Tate, Brielle, Daisy, and Hunter were all out to breakfast, and Nate had the day off. I happened to find my way into Nate's bedroom for a late morning session.

He held me close, our eyes closed, as we just lay together. It felt so good to be in his arms. It felt right.

The comforter cocooned us as the spring weather fought with winter, and a late April snow made its way to the ground.

I heard a funny noise and opened my eyes to see two large nostrils steaming up Nate's bedroom window.

My body shook with laughter as I elbowed Nate and watched Lucky staring right at us.

"She doesn't look too happy," I whispered.

"Who? What?" Nate asked, shifting in bed to see. "What in the world?"

Nate grabbed the sheet and wrapped it around himself, then flew out of bed to pull the blinds down.

"You made yourself decent for the mule?"

Nate spun around, his eyes connecting with mine, and smiled. "You have no idea what Millie did to that mule. You know how you teased that she'd imprinted on me?"

My brows rose. "Yeah?"

"Well, she did. Lucky is... Lucky is in love with me."

I giggled, pushing down the comforter with my feet. "Okay, Nate. Whatever you say."

"It's the truth. How else would you explain this?" He raised the blinds again to have Lucky's big brown eyes still staring inside.

I smiled at Nate, realizing that even though he was a big hulk of a man, a sheriff, and an incredible boyfriend, he still had his eccentricities, and I loved him even more for it.

His eyes scanned over my body and stopped at the little crocheted bandeau top and boy shorts I had on from the bazaar. "Those are really cute."

"Thanks." It was nice to have a reason to wear them.

Nate pulled on his pants and tugged a sweater over his head. "I'll go get her secured, and then I should head out to meet with Tom."

"Okay, sounds good." I stretched toward the ceiling and slowly yawned as Nate walked into the bathroom.

I followed him and hung on to the door. "Are you feeling okay about this meeting?"

Nate smiled and looked over at me as he styled his hair. "Yeah. I am. I think, no matter the outcome, it will be good. I still can't help but feel remorse, but I'm understanding your perspective a little bit more each day."

I moved into the bathroom and slid a kiss across Nate's cheek. "Thanks for letting me in, Sheriff. We do good for each other."

His laugh rumbled through the bathroom as I turned on the shower. "You've got to wait until I leave, or it will start all over again."

I smiled and shook my head. "Learn some self-control, Nate."

"That's the problem, Amy. With you, I have none."

His familiar, fun-loving smirk slid across his face as he pulled me into him for another kiss.

I felt so close to Nate now, and it was as if each day just strengthened our bond. Nate's hug loosened, and he stepped away as I got into the shower and drew a heart onto the glass through the steam.

"For me?" he teased.

"Am I making the sheriff blush?"

He laughed and shook his head. "Not any more than Lucky."

I rolled my eyes. "Whatever, tough guy. You know I can drop you to your knees."

A thought occurred to me. "You know, I've been meaning to ask you something."

"Anything." He pulled a black knit hat over his head as I rinsed the shampoo out of my hair.

"What did Leo say to you in the car ride before you dropped him off?"

The air between us stilled, and silence filled the room for a few seconds before Nate walked over. "Leo told me that he could tell I loved you, and he asked if he was right."

My heart pounded faster as I opened my eyes to see Nate's.

"And I told him that I loved you." He took a deep

breath and let it out. "So he asked me to take care of you. He told me you deserved a good life more than anyone. He didn't say another word."

My hands started trembling, but I kept them tangled in my hair so Nate couldn't see.

"Wow," I said, pushing down the tightness in my throat.

"Even with all of this stuff, Amy," Nate said softly, "he does love you. It's his disease."

I closed my eyes and let the shower water rinse my tears away so Nate didn't see them. I didn't want him to be late to meet Tom.

"See you in a bit, Amy. I love you."

"Love you too," I told him as he walked out of the bathroom. Tears continued to stream down my face, and I thought about the man Leo had become.

It wasn't fair what happened to him. He could have turned out like Alice and me. He could have been happy with a bright future.

I never could have loved him how he wanted me to, but I know I could have led him to the love he should have had.

My mind fell back to the Sunshine Breakfast Club. Maybe that was how it all started, like Millie said. All it takes is a smidge of love.

The tears stopped as I rinsed off the rest of the soap and stepped out of the shower. The truth of it was that I did still love Leo as a friend, but I knew I couldn't save him. He had to want it himself. And I hated to admit it, but maybe the trouble he got himself into was a cry for help.

My gut told me he knew I wouldn't play along. Maybe it was his way of throwing up his hands, rolling the dice, and seeing what happens next.

He'd be in jail for long enough to get clean, but with my heart of hearts, I hoped he could stay that way.

I glanced at myself in the mirror as I pulled up my underwear and clasped my bra. I liked what I saw for the first time in a long time. My dark golden blonde hair, which seemed light brown in today's lighting, shimmered, and the glow of my cheeks made me feel alive. I didn't bother with makeup and just pulled on a sweatshirt. I didn't feel like a mess any longer.

Correction.

I felt like an understood mess.

My thoughts still flew all over the place about the town I grew up in, my parents and their choices, and Leo, but I now had someone I could talk to without feeling uncomfortable.

As much as Nate had been talking to me over the last week, I knew he felt the same. Once I chipped away those walls, it was like he turned into a floodgate of dreams, hopes, and regrets, and I loved hearing every single thing.

But I knew above all else that Nate was my forever, and the Sunshine Breakfast Club was good at what they did.

The weird part was that as I roamed the town this week and spotted someone without a ring on their finger, my own fingers would tingle, and my mind would start racing with matches.

It was contagious.

Millie was right. It was... a feeling.

But I was due back to Brielle's in about twenty minutes since she'd be getting home with Tate soon.

I clipped my hair into a barrette and made my way to the window where smudge marks remained from Lucky's steaming nostrils. At least she didn't try to knock me down or kick me. I think we had a mutual understanding of sorts. I'd take care of Nate inside, and she'd give him hell outside.

I rounded everything up and headed out the door to make the trip to the lake house. The drive was easy, with the snowflakes trading to sunshine and the snow melting.

When I pulled into the driveway, Brielle's rear was sticking out of the car as she tried to unfasten Tate. I quickly unbuckled and rushed to help. For some reason, Brielle and car seats never turned out well.

"Hey, Brielle. Was breakfast fun?"

Brielle sighed and climbed out of her luxury SUV with an exasperated look, glanced at me with a smile, and said, "It was delightful, and Tate was such a little doll. I hate being away from him."

"I can only imagine." I reached and unfastened him from the car seat and stepped aside so Brielle could lift him into her arms.

"It's awful, and I told Nick that even though I love staying with him on these long trips, I need to be home with Tate more. I just can't handle it. That's what we were hashing out over breakfast."

My heart skipped. *Oh, no.* Would she be in Chicago more? Would that be where she expected me to be?

We walked up to the house, and I opened the door.

"I can't believe I'm saying this, but I'll be at the Chicago house."

My heart stopped. "And then come up when it's my time to see Tate. I can see he loves it here. Everyone loves him to death. He's like a little celebrity."

Relief spread through me at an unstoppable speed. "Yeah, he's pretty much everyone's favorite little boy."

"I know we don't get to talk much, but I really wanted you to know how much Nick, Daisy, Hunter, and I appreciate you."

I was stunned at her gratitude. Somehow, I was usually the one thanking her.

"He's an angel, and I feel so blessed to have come into this family to work." I smiled, glancing out at the lake that had completely defrosted. The glistening of the water shimmered the sun's rays back into the world, and I couldn't help but feel lucky to be here. "It's been a privilege, and I've really gotten to experience some amazing things."

"I heard a little rumor that you and the sheriff might be having a fling."

Just the mention of Nate lit up my world, and I couldn't hide my smile as Brielle bounced Tate on her lap in the family room.

"I hope it's more than that."

And I did hope that. With all of my heart.

Brielle nodded thoughtfully as she turned her attention back to Tate. She set him on the floor, and he started playing with toys I'd forgotten to put away.

"Word on the street is that he's very fond of you," Brielle said knowingly.

I chuckled, thinking back to this morning when he

was extremely fond of all parts of me.

"It's funny," I told her. "When you and Nick asked me to come here and be the nanny for Tate in Buttercup Lake, I was crushed. It felt like all my big city dreams had been smashed."

"Oh, really?" Brielle said, glancing at me.

I nodded. "Yeah, and then I got here and fell in love. I couldn't imagine living anywhere else."

Brielle laughed, throwing her head back. "There is something about this place that just grows on you."

"You don't sound too happy about it," I teased.

"I'm just resigned." She grinned, leaning down to play with her son. "Life has a way of weaving you back to the people and places that need you most or who you need."

Brielle looked up at me and smiled. "And I know Tate needs Buttercup Lake. I wouldn't want him to grow up anywhere else."

"Really?"

She nodded. "Yeah. It just seems like the best place for him."

"I agree."

My mind slipped back to Nate, and I hoped with everything that his conversation with Tom was going better than expected.

Chapter Twenty-Eight

Nate

I spotted Tom sitting on the patio outside the restaurant. He had an iced tea that he sipped as I made my way over. When he spotted me, he tugged on his baseball cap and slipped off his shades.

The tension in my chest vanished the moment he smiled.

He stood up and reached out a hand. "Good to see you, Nate." He smiled and took his seat again. "I wasn't sure if you were going to come in your uniform or what."

I smiled, nodding. "Yeah. It's my day off."

Tom looked exactly like he had in college. His blond hair flipped up along the edge of his baseball hat, and his lean frame still signaled that he ran.

"I don't even know where to begin," Tom said, stirring the ice in his tea.

I nodded slowly as the server came over to take my drink order. She walked away, and I brought my attention back to Tom.

Frown lines etched Tom's mouth, and my stomach knotted.

"When I got your email about Ella's memorial bench, I lost it."

My shoulders rolled back, and I straightened in the chair. "I'm sorry about that." I dropped my gaze to the metal table and took a deep breath.

Tom shook his head. "No, Nate. That's the thing. You shouldn't be saying sorry about any of this. None of it."

My eyes flashed to Tom's, and I shook my head. "What do you mean? I know your family hates me, and I don't blame them one bit, and then our friendship imploded…" I shook my head, circling the napkin in front of me as the server brought my drink. "And I get it. I get it all. I can't even imagine the grief and sorrow you've had to endure. I know what I've felt, and it's a mere fraction."

"But that's our burden, Nate. Not yours."

I shook my head. "Not how I see it."

"Nate, you asked me for forgiveness, and there's

nothing to forgive." His eyes stayed on mine. "I want you to know that. When my mom heard that you've been blaming yourself, she broke down. You're such a kind-hearted guy. You always have been."

My mind raced with questions. *Then why did I get dumped? Treated like I had the plague?*

My pulse felt like a drumbeat of anticipation as the patio filled up with the lunch crowd.

"I'm truly sorry, Tom. There's not a day that goes by when I don't think of your sister and that night. I wished I'd handled things differently."

Tom shook his head. "Do you know when I felt the closest to you?"

"When?"

"That night, as she was leaving, I realized my best friend had done the right thing. Do you know how many guys would have taken advantage of that situation, used my sister, and discarded her? You did the right thing, Nate. You always have."

"But if I'd—"

Tom interrupted me, shaking his head. "No, Nate. That's the thing. We can't go back in time. We can't change things we wish we could." His fingers clenched into a tight ball, and he shook his head, looking over the lake. "I loved this place. I thought I'd come back from college and figure out a way to support myself, raise a family, the whole bit. Remember?"

"I do." *And I blew that for you.*

"But the thing is, Nate, we can't change the past. It's a realization that took me over a decade to understand. I only wish I knew you'd been beating yourself up for all these years so we could have done it together."

I shook my head, not understanding. "What do you mean?"

"I'm the one who bought her that bottle of vodka. She said it was for a party." He moved his fingers through his hair and sucked in a breath. "I thought it seemed innocent enough, kind of like the stuff you and I'd get away with back in high school. I figured sneaking a little booze to my little sister was better than some of the stuff going around, and she'd be the hit of her class."

The admission hung in the air as if it didn't know where to hide.

I sat stunned in disbelief. I didn't know what to say, so I said absolutely nothing.

"So, when I got your email, I just felt... sick." He shook his head. "I figured you'd moved on. That was what I'd hoped, anyway."

I nodded, realizing how little we knew of people sometimes.

"There were times when I thought about ending things," he said softly, bringing his eyes to mine. "But I couldn't do that to my parents. They'd already lost Ella."

"Did they know?" I asked. "About the booze?"

He shook his head. "No one does. Not until today."

"Wow." I shook my head. "I'm just so sorry."

"No, Nate. I'm sorry for being a lousy friend. I was so lost, and anything that reminded me of Ella made me have to think about what I'd done. What I'd handed her. I couldn't do it. I wanted to reach out to you so many times over the last decade, but I figured you'd moved on and probably had no interest."

"Not true." I shook my head.

"Yeah. I gathered that." He ran his fingers along the stubble on his jaw and scratched his chin. "I want you to know that if you had handled that night any other way, I wouldn't be sitting here right now. You were and are an amazing friend."

"Thank you, Tom. I appreciate that."

"It's the truth, Nate. You need to stop blaming yourself for something that was out of your control."

"What about you?" I asked.

His gaze dipped to the lake, and he shook his head. "See? That's the difference. It was fully within my control."

"You're not the first brother to buy their younger siblings booze, and you won't be the last." I shook my head. "Believe me, I see it all the time."

Tom brought his gaze to mine and nodded. "Thank you for still considering a memorial to Ella. At the time when your uncle offered it, things were too fresh, and it probably sounds crazy, but it was like we didn't want any reminders that she'd passed away, you know? It was almost like we could fool ourselves into pretending she hadn't."

I nodded.

"But it's time. Ella deserves that. She deserved it long ago, and I want to share my story so that, hopefully, other kids don't fall into the same trap I did, wanting to be the cool sibling."

"That would be incredible, man," I said, reaching over to tap his shoulder.

But instead, he stood up and reached his arms out. "Hug?"

I laughed, thinking back to when we were kids, and wondered if it could ever be close to that one day.

"Still as bony as hell," I said, laughing, slapping his back as we hugged.

"At least I won't get mistaken for a meatloaf with legs."

I laughed, letting go as we both sat down, not saying anything more for several minutes.

Instead, we let Buttercup Lake sparkle in the background, working hard to mend the friendship that we'd both let slip away.

I took a sip of iced tea and looked over at Tom. "Never did I think I'd experience this again."

His brows arched as his eyes met mine. "Oh, yeah?"

I smiled, nodding. "How's your mom and dad?"

"Honestly, we never really returned to being the same, but how could we?" He shrugged. "A piece of us had been taken away, and the way we had to return to fill that void just isn't the same. My parents are still together, thankfully. They poured themselves into the family business. I know there are days my mom doesn't want to get out of bed, but she still does."

"I'm just so sorry."

Tom nodded.

"You said you wanted to tell your part of the story, but I'm the only person who knows. What about your parents? How are they going to take it?"

Tom clenched his fingers together. "I honestly don't

know, but I need to tell them."

"You're doing a brave thing, Tom."

He let out a cynical laugh. "After a decade or more of being a coward?"

I shook my head, realizing we all had a part to play, and none of us could know what the other participant in this game of life was dealt. I never, ever put two and two together that Tom was the one who'd supplied the liquor. It didn't make me look at Tom any differently. Why would it? But it told me that Amy was right.

I could finally breathe again.

And I felt truly humbled that Tom chose me to tell, and I think that spoke to our friendship.

"I'll always be here for you, man." I shook my head. "Always."

"I wish all this time hadn't gone by."

I nodded. "Me too. But I think it was meant to be."

"That doesn't sound like the Nate I know." He eyed me.

"I've softened recently. I even shared feelings."

Tom laughed. "With whom?"

"A girl."

"Does this girl have a name?"

"Amy Nichols. She's a nanny for a family here in

town."

"She's *The One*, isn't she?"

"How'd you know?"

"I can see it in your eyes." Tom nodded. "Nice, man. Really nice."

"Thanks. It's pretty recent. Just this year. We met in December and didn't really start dating until February."

"Wow. And you already know?" He looked surprised.

"Without a shadow of a doubt. She's my girl. I can tell her anything, and she's actually the first person I told about Ella."

Tom gave me a knowing look. "Yeah. She's the one."

"Hey, would you like to meet her?"

"Yeah. Sure. What the heck? I'm staying overnight."

I slid my phone out of my pocket and texted Amy to see if she'd like to visit, and she responded right back.

"Shoot. She's on nanny duty. Maybe we can catch some dinner later and you can meet her?"

"Absolutely."

I nodded and texted back, and she agreed just as Millie walked onto the patio with her great-granddaughter.

I gave a quick wave, and Millie stopped instantly, recognizing Tom.

"Tom, it's so good to see you," she said, wandering

over with Izzy right behind.

Tom stood up and hugged Millie. "You look great. Not a day over forty."

Millie giggled and shook her head. "I hope you move back here soon. You married? Got a girlfriend?"

Tom laughed and shook his head. "Nope. Single as can be, but I know about your little book club. There's no way I'd fall for it."

She feigned innocence as Izzy chuckled. "This town is full of good readers. Their comprehension of the material is unmistakable." She turned to me and pointed. "In fact, I got Nate his happily-ever-after just like I did with your parents, Tom."

My gaze flashed to Tom. "What? This group infiltrated your parents?"

Tom nodded. "Yeah. My mom told me about that a few years ago. I guess my mom got dragged to some book club by her mom back in the day, and Millie was behind it. Next thing you know, my dad is proposing to my mom."

"I had no idea."

Tom chuckled and looked at me. "Well, I can't wait to meet Amy."

"She's amazing."

"I second that," Izzy said. "But I'm starving."

"Oh, and Nate," Millie said. "I'm glad you worked things out with Amy on your own. I wasn't really sure what you wanted our little book club to do."

I laughed, shaking my head. "Oh, Millie. You and Lucky are not off the hook. Just wait. There'll be a time when your services are requested."

Millie winked at me. "If you say so. By the way, your dad's over at the clinic. I guess he threw out his back."

I frowned. "Again?"

She nodded and laughed. "I overheard him telling the doctor your mom was wearing some skimpy crocheted number, and one thing led to another..."

I held up my hand in horror. "Okay, Millie. I get it. Thanks for that visual."

"Well, I'm just saying that the lady who makes them is local. Maybe Amy would like one."

I glared at Millie. "She already has one, Millie, and I'm beginning to think you and Lucky are in cahoots."

"What are you, crazy? I don't speak mule." She wandered away, and I realized I'd never be able to escape this crazy town, and that was okay because I never really wanted to.

Chapter Twenty-Nine

One Year Later

Amy

I slid my hands along the pearls and lace and closed my eyes, smelling the sweet smell of fresh-cut lawn. A string quartet played, the music humming softly in the background as I looked around the cherry orchard.

Nate's parents happily agreed to let us get married on their farm, and that time was almost here.

I was hiding behind a hedge of roses the florists brought in, but I managed a glimpse of Nate as he slowly walked down the aisle, looking so handsome and stoic.

Boy, did I love that man.

"You look gorgeous," Daisy whispered, handing me

the bouquet as Abby signaled it was their time to walk down the aisle with the groomsmen.

Even the air zipped with magic as I looked around the beautiful setting. Daisy winked at me as Hunter looped his arm through hers. The music changed, and I felt like I was being spun into a fairytale, creating a reality that couldn't exist.

But it was all real.

A profound sense of reality pulsed through me as I snuck a peak at our bridal party, marching down the aisle. I spotted my parents sitting in the front row, and I smiled. They were who they were, and I couldn't change it. Luckily, my dad didn't take it hard at all when I told my parents that Alice would be walking me down the aisle.

My sister bounced over and squeezed my hand in excitement. "You ready for this? You look absolutely beautiful."

I drew a breath as I turned to Brielle and nodded for Tate to make his way as our ring bearer. She grinned and helped him down the aisle, where Hunter waited at the other end. Tate went into full-speed mode, waddling quickly with the white satin pillow forgotten along the way.

The guests chuckled, and Brielle couldn't help but smile.

I turned to the mule and patted her neck. "Okay, Lucky. Show us what you got."

"I can't believe you're letting a donkey be your flower girl."

"She's a mule, and she's family." I nosed Lucky, who gave a little twitch of agreement as Brielle reappeared with the pillow.

"Maybe Lucky will have a better chance of getting this to the groom." Brielle slid it under Lucky's satin harness, and I heard Nate give a quick little whistle.

On command, Lucky threw one last look at me before she started down the aisle, and I suddenly wondered if she thought she was the bride.

"This is so bizarre." Alice chuckled and handed me a beautiful bouquet filled with peonies, hydrangeas, and baby roses as I watched Lucky make it down to Hunter.

Tom stepped forward and removed the ring pillow before leading Lucky to the side where Millie stood with her reins.

As the music changed, my pulse soared, and my heart fluttered with anticipation.

I was about to marry the man of my dreams.

"You ready?" Alice whispered.

"Absolutely."

As we took our first step from behind the hedge, the guests stood, and Nate kept his gaze fastened on me. It was like the world fell away as I walked slowly down the aisle to the tempo of the music. It was hard to believe that so many of our friends and family had gathered for this intimate moment.

Magic filled the air as I made my way closer to Nate. Our eyes never left one another's, and I knew I'd found my home.

When we reached Nate, my sister looked at him and smiled. "Take good care of my sister, Sheriff."

He smiled and nodded. "With all my heart, I will."

I looked at my row of bridesmaids where Daisy, Abby, Jill, and Leo stood.

His eyes connected with mine, and he gave me a short nod of approval.

He'd been nine months sober, and I couldn't have asked for anything more than to have him part of my day.

I brought my gaze to Nate's, who held my hands in his.

He whispered a quick *I love you*, and I did the same.

The pastor began talking about love, but I didn't need to be told about it. I'd already felt it. I knew what it was to be loved by a man and accepted wholly by someone just for being me. He not only accepted my past but also praised the hurdles that created the person I became.

And I did the same for him. I couldn't imagine Nate being Nate if it weren't for Tom. These two men had blamed themselves far too long for a world they couldn't control. I looked over at Leo and smiled.

Him too.

Three very different outcomes for three very different men.

"Would you like to recite your vows now, Nate?" the pastor asked.

His eyes sparkled as he held my hands even tighter.

"I find myself at a loss for words when I think about what you've brought to my life, Lucky." He glanced at the mule behind me, and the guests chuckled. "But I mean it, Amy. I never knew that my life could change so drastically yet remain the same in so many ways when I found my person. You've enchanted me with your knowledge, compassion, forgiving spirit, and insight."

"I told myself I wouldn't cry," I whispered, taking a hand away from his to wipe away a tear.

"You've made me a complete person, Amy. I'm not scared to embrace my past and let it guide my future. You've allowed me to open my heart, and I think it's made me a better man. I don't want to spend another day in this world without you as my wife."

He bent over and swiped a kiss on my lips as the pastor cleared his throat.

"Not yet," the pastor said, laughing.

"Amy, do you have vows you'd like to share?"

I nodded and kept my gaze on Nate's as his words still swirled around me. I didn't know how I lucked out in this world to find my person, but I couldn't imagine taking one step forward without him any longer.

"Nate, from the moment you met me, I bared more than just my soul to you," I said softly as Millie giggled behind us. Nate smirked and shook his head. "But in all seriousness, I never in my wildest dreams knew I could find a man who loved as hard as you do, who allows me to be me and praises me for it, who accepts all my baggage and helps me gather more. You are the most giving man I've ever met, and I can't thank you enough for allowing me into your world, all of it. I can't wait to spend the rest of my life with you."

Nate shook his head, but his eyes stayed locked on mine. I felt butterflies colliding in my belly as the familiar little smirk appeared on his delicious lips.

He leaned over and kissed me again, and warmth spread through me as the pastor scolded us again.

The pastor looked over the crowd of friends and

family, at Lucky, and now Millie, who was somehow sitting on top of our mule, and smiled.

"It's with great pleasure that I introduce the Sunshine Breakfast Club's latest match. You may now kiss the bride."

Nate took me in his arms and dipped me as his mouth met mine, and I knew it all started with a smidge of love. We nurtured it, fought for it, and most importantly, wanted it.

And it felt good to be seen.

Dear Readers,

Thank you so much for allowing Buttercup Lake and the Sunshine Breakfast Club to be part of your world. I can say that after I finish writing each book in the series, I'm just happy. These characters and stories just leave me smiling, and I hope these stories do the same for you!

I don't know if you noticed the mention of Honey Leaf Lodge throughout this story, but the lodge is actually the start of a new series for me! It's going to be based in this same world but follow different characters. Characters from the Sunshine Breakfast Club will hop in from time to time too. If you'd like something to read until then, the Curiosity Bay Series is my newest, and I've provided a little excerpt below from Heart of Curiosities.

Don't forget to sign up for my newsletter at my website or follow me on Facebook to learn when more of Buttercup Lake, Sunshine Breakfast Club, and the Honey Leaf Lodge will be here!

Many thanks for reading all about Nate and Amy. I hope you loved them! I sure did.

Warmest wishes,

Karice

BOOKS BY KARICE BOLTON

CURIOSITY BAY SERIES
Heart of Curiosities
Wilds of the Heart
Tempting the Heart

THE SUNSHINE BREAKFAST CLUB SERIES
DASH OF LOVE
PINCH OF LOVE
SPRINKLE OF LOVE
CHRISTMAS OF LOVE
SMIDGE OF LOVE

CLOUDBERRY INN SERIES
IMAGINING YOU
REMEMBERING YOU
LEAVING YOU
LOVING YOU

ISLAND COUNTY SERIES
FINDING LOVE IN FORGOTTEN COVE
LOVE REDONE IN HIDDEN HARBOR
TANGLED LOVE ON PELICAN POINT
FOREVER LOVE ON FIREWEED ISLAND
TEMPTING LOVE ON HOLLY LANE
CHANCE AT LOVE ON MYSTIC BAY
IRRESISTIBLE LOVE AT SILVER FALLS
LUCKY IN LOVE ON HOUND ISLAND
MISTLETOE MISCHIEF
ACCIDENTAL LOVE ON MEADOW COVE LANE
DISCOVERING LOVE ON CRANBERRY LANE
CHRISTMAS ON FIREWEED
IMAGINING LOVE ON WILLOW ROAD
CHRISTMAS CRUSH ON FIREWEED ISLAND

WAITING LOVE AT HAWTHORNE AVENUE
FOREVER CHRISTMAS ON SUGARPLUM LANE

BEYOND LOVE SERIES
BEYOND CONTROL
BEYOND DOUBT
BEYOND REASON
BEYOND INTENT
BEYOND CHANCE
BEYOND PROMISE
BEYOND the MISTLETOE

SILVER RIDGE SERIES
A HAPPY TRUTH ABOUT LOVE
A LITTLE SECRET ABOUT LOVE
A FUNNY THING ABOUT LOVE
A SURPRISING FACT ABOUT LOVE
A SIMPLE WISH ABOUT LOVE
CHRISTMAS AT SILVER RIDGE

LUKE FLETCHER SERIES
HIDDEN SINS
BURIED SINS
REDEMPTION
MIA

V MAFIA SERIES
BLAKE
DEVIN
JAXSON

SECRETS AMONG US

THE WITCH AVENUE SERIES
LONELY SOULS
ALTERED SOULS

SMIDGE OF LOVE

RELEASED SOULS
SHATTERED SOULS

THE WATCHERS TRILOGY
AWAKENING
LEGIONS
CATACLYSM
TAKEN NOVELLA (A Watchers Prequel)

AFTERWORLD SERIES
RecruitZ
AlibiZ
UprisingZ

BLOOD TORN DUET
BLOOD TORN
BLOOD CURSED